ANYWHERE *with* YOU

A ROMANTIC COMEDY

CHRISTINA ELLE

ABOUT ANYWHERE WITH YOU

You are cordially invited . . . to tick off the bride.

Teegan Michaels has attended six weddings for her sorority sisters dateless and she refuses to go to the last one alone. Not when she has a perfectly respectable—not to mention hot—NFL player ready to save her from humiliation. Who cares that he's the bride's ex-fiancé and only wants to go for revenge? What's the worst that could happen?

Edited by Alchemy and Words
Cover and Interior Design by Uplifting Designs
Cover art from Deposit Photos
First edition May 2018

DEDICATION

To Misty. Without her, I would've given up on this dream a long time ago.

And to Keith. You might not be as tall as JJ Watt. Or have as many muscles. Or play professional football. But you're mine and I love you.

ANYWHERE *with* YOU

A ROMANTIC COMEDY

Chapter One

Teegan Michaels sat at her usual booth by the window at the small New York City café, sipping black coffee.

The bell above the front door rang louder than normal, attracting Teegan's attention. She looked up and watched her best friend, Misty Stevenson-Hue, barrel in. "Sorry I'm late. Major meltdown in the Hue house today."

Misty's frizzy, chin-length auburn hair stuck out in every direction, but that was nothing new. Poor thing was habitually sleep deprived and rarely took the few seconds she did have in the morning to comb her hair.

"Are the girls okay?" Teegan asked with a frown.

Misty snorted as she slid into the booth, dropping her purse and unwrapping her plaid scarf. "The girls? Please. Jim had the meltdown—he was afraid to be left home alone with them."

Teegan laughed. Misty and Jim had two-year-old twin daughters. Lately, it had been attack of the hellions at their place.

"He called three times while I was on my way here," she said, pulling the extra coffee Teegan had ordered toward her like it was the Holy Grail. She reached for her bag, rooted around inside, and pulled out a small silver container. Unscrewing the top, she poured a steady stream of amber liquid into the steaming cup.

Oh, it was *that* kind of day.

Smiling, Teegan said, "You should've told me it was bring-your-flask-to-work day. I would've dressed up for the occasion."

Misty blew out a breath, tipping the canister up to cut off the flow. "I've been counting down the minutes till I could have this. It's been so crazy at home. Jim's schedule has gotten worse. He's gone nearly three weeks out of the month now. When he's home, I feel like all I do is toss the girls at him and run out the door for a few hours of sanity." She flipped an errant curl out of her eyes. "Life between the sheets hasn't been all that great lately, either. Foreplay now includes him asking if I want to watch *Game of Thrones* or *The Walking Dead*. It's pathetic. I can't freaking wait to get away for a while. We need this time together."

Misty sipped her drink, then pulled it away and looked down at it with disgust. She picked up the flask and poured more liquor into her cup. After swallowing another dose, she licked her lips and nodded as if satisfied. "Speaking of which, how's it going? You get a date for this wedding yet or what?"

Teegan groaned, knowing that would be answer enough.

"Nothing worked? Not even that website Jessica told us about?"

"I don't believe I'm going to find a date for a destination wedding on an app where you have to swipe left or right based on how hot someone looks in their profile picture."

Shrugging, Misty said, "Time's running out. Either you call Juliet and tell her to remove your plus one, or you suck it up and get flexible." She pointed out the window. "Oh, look. That guy looks nice."

Teegan followed her line of sight to a tall man wearing a khaki trench coat and dress pants, carrying a briefcase. He was cute. Dark hair. Put together. Looked sensible. She lowered her gaze, as she was accustomed to doing lately. "The thick gold band on his left hand looks nice too."

Misty squinted. "Yeah. That sucks."

"Mmm-hmm." Story of her life. The men she typically met were married, players, or psychopaths. At least, one of the men seemed like he had psychopathic tendencies. That date had been a quick one.

She dropped her head forward, thudding it against the table several times. "Why did I tell Juliet I was bringing a date?"

"Because you're tired of going to our sorority sisters' weddings stag. How many has it been now? Four? Five?" Teegan lifted her head just high enough to watch Misty counting on her fingers. "There was Hillary, Samara was next, followed by Katie...oh, and Saylor." Misty seemed stuck on the last two names, so Teegan helped her out.

"Jessica and Avery." Sighing, Teegan sat up straight and wrapped her hands around her warm mug. "Six, Misty. I've gone to six weddings dateless."

With sad puppy eyes and a sympathetic smile, Misty offered her flask.

Teegan snatched it and poured enough to fill her nearly empty coffee back up. "That has to be some sort of record, right? I mean, whose luck is that bad? Or is it even luck? I think it might be me. I'm doing something to literally repel men."

Misty tapped her finger against her cheek in thought. "I bet we could turn this into a positive. We should call Guinness Book and tell them about—"

Teegan cut off her friend's statement with a peeved look, then said, "I won't attend another wedding alone. I have to find someone. I'm so desperate, I've been considering paying a man to be my date."

Misty slammed her cup onto the table, sloshing a huge splash of whiskey and black coffee onto the battered wood table. Her eyes were wide and excited. "What, like an escort? Oh my God. Can I help pick him? Please? Please? Please?"

"I didn't say I was going to hire someone. Just that I thought about it."

Things weren't that bad. Yet.

Misty slumped into the seat on her side of the booth. A few seconds later, she held up a finger and offered, "There's another option, you know. Not sure if you're up for it though."

Thank goodness. Hopefully, this alternative option wasn't too pricey. "Let's hear it."

Misty's phone rang. She didn't glance at her purse where the loud tune was coming from. Instead, she kept her gaze on Teegan. "Part of me wants to let the call go to voicemail. The other part is afraid the girls have tied Jim up, and they're calling for ransom."

Poor guy.

"You better get it."

Digging her hand inside the oversize mom bag, Misty pulled out her phone and looked at the screen. "Oh, it's Wes."

Misty's older brother. Extra tall, broad, and muscular. Every girl in college had drooled over Wes. Teegan wasn't going to lie and say she'd never fantasized about him. Wes was hot with a capital *H* but he didn't seem to realize his devastating hotness. Or maybe he just didn't care that he made panties melt by walking past. Instead, he was the type to see a lonely girl on the perimeter of the dance floor and asked her to dance simply because he was that nice. He'd come to Teegan's rescue more than a few times at college formals or dateless weddings. He might've been with Juliet back then, but he always insisted on saving a dance for Teegan.

Yep—melting panties all over the place.

Misty swiped a finger across her phone's screen. "Damn. I missed it." She placed the device on the table beside her coffee. "I'll call him back in the cab."

"You sure?" Teegan asked. "I don't mind."

Waving the comment away, Misty said, "It's fine. I know what he's calling about anyway."

"How's Wes doing?" Teegan knew he was living in Texas after his pro football career ended prematurely due to an injury. If she remembered correctly, his only partner in life now was his bullmastiff named Peanut.

Teegan might've been keeping track.

Didn't matter though. Misty had made it clear that she wouldn't support any of her friends dating her brother ever again—not after Juliet had broken his heart.

Misty lifted her mug and sipped again. "I haven't had a chance to tell you. He got some amazing news from the doc last week."

"Oh yeah?"

"Yeah, he got released off the DL."

Disabled list. Something Teegan had heard was impossible based on the severity of his injury.

"But I thought you said the ACL was completely torn. That it would take months and months of surgery and therapy before he'd even be able to jog."

Misty's eyes brightened as her smile disappeared behind her lifted mug. "You know Wes is a stubborn ass. If there's something he wants, he's single-minded about getting it." She shrugged. "He wanted off the gimp squad—as he called it—and to play football again, so he did it."

Wow. Teegan had to give him credit. There wasn't much in her life that important to fight for. Not that things came easy for her. She worked hard to earn a decent living and pay for her one-bedroom apartment in Manhattan, but she'd never been so down and out, craving for something everyone told her would never happen.

"That's amazing. I remember you telling me how impossible the doctors said a comeback would be. Good for him."

Misty's expression showed her elation for her brother's hard work. "I'm so proud of that big lump of a man. It's not public yet, so don't say anything to anyone. He wants it to be a surprise." A wide, delighted smirk spread across her face. "Juliet's going to be so freakin' shocked when she finds out. God, I hope I get to see her reaction."

Her phone rang again. She lowered her eyes to the screen then shook her head and grinned.

"Persistent as hell." Misty pressed a button, making the cell go silent. Looking at Teegan, she said, "Him again."

"You can answer it," Teegan said. "I don't mind. He's called twice. Something might be wrong. What if Jim is in trouble and he can't get a hold of you, so he called Wes to reach you?"

Still smiling, Misty dropped her chin and lifted her eyebrows.

"Okay, probably not," Teegan said. "But, obviously, he needs you right now if he keeps calling."

"It's not me he needs," she said. "It's you."

Teegan? What could Wes possibly need from her?

Misty's phone started ringing again. She smirked, pressed a button to answer the call and handed the device across the table.

Hesitantly, Teegan took the phone and placed it to her ear, attempting to keep her racing heart in check. She'd known Wes for years, and he still made her nervous. He was always so put together and poised. Unlike Teegan, who felt like a bumbling idiot whenever she talked to him.

"H-hello?" she said.

"Hey, Teegan." The delight in his voice gave her a small start. "It's Wes."

"Oh, Wes," she said through a nervous laugh, like she didn't already know it was him. She flicked her gaze up to Misty, who was watching her with sharp eyes and a quirk to one side of her lips. "How are you?"

"Great, thanks. How about you?"

She swallowed past her dry throat. "G-good."

There was a long, awkward pause. Then he cleared his throat on the other end. "I'm calling because I need a favor."

"Favor? From me?" Teegan was trying to be cool, she really was, but she was shaking all the way down to her bones.

"Actually, it's more than just a favor. I need a date."

"*What?*" All the oxygen in her lungs emptied in half a second. She was sure her face was deep red. A quick glance at Misty, whose smirk had widened to the wattage of a lit Christmas tree, confirmed Teegan's thoughts.

This was a man who was swarmed by hundreds of women simply walking to the grocery store. He hardly needed Teegan's help in the dating department.

"I want you to take me as your date to Juliet's wedding," he went on, confidence in his tone.

She choked on her tongue. "You want me to do *what*?"

Looking across the table, Misty was still grinning behind her spiked coffee.

"I want to be your date for Juliet's wedding," Wes said. "It's not a big deal. You need a date, right? I'll do it."

"But...but Juliet is your ex. You guys lived together. You-you slept together." Wildly and passionately, according to Juliet.

There was a grunt on the other end, then, "Yeah. And you remember what happened after."

She did. Juliet had left him while he was rehabbing from his injury, after he was released from his team. They were engaged, and she just up and left him. Wes. The best guy out there.

"If you were already going with someone, I wouldn't ask," he said. "But Misty mentioned that you were still dateless, so I thought...I figured..."

She propped an elbow on the table and rubbed her forehead. "That I'd be desperate?"

"Yes. No. I mean, I assumed you'd want to go with someone. Anyone."

God, had it gotten so bad that even Misty's hot older brother—who lived thousands of miles away, mind you—knew she was pathetically single?

"I don't know, Wes," she said, garnering a confused look from her friend.

Why? Misty mouthed. *What's wrong?*

"I just..." she went on. "I'm afraid what people would say." She'd never been fully accepted by her Delta Gamma sisters. Sure, she was one of them. But she'd always felt like she was on the outside looking in. That was never more apparent when they all were happy in love, and she was…not.

What would they think of her if she took the bride's ex to the wedding? It screamed of desperation, didn't it?

A frustrated sigh came from the other end. "Look, Teegan. I know you won't understand, but I need this. I *need* to be at that wedding."

His voice was fierce and unrelenting. The passion behind his words was unmistakable.

"Why?" she asked. "So you can ruin her wedding? Toss her fiancé into the ocean to be eaten by sharks?"

"Hmm, that's a great plan."

"You—" she started as her mouth dropped open.

"I'm joking," Wes said. "I have no idea what I'm going to do. I haven't gotten that far. I just need Juliet to see me one last time, whole, getting around like I was never hurt. I want her to regret leaving me."

As far as anyone else was concerned, Juliet had made an enormous mistake. Wes was an amazing man. Sweet, caring, talented, and giving. He was damn near perfect. Someone Teegan would love the hell out of if ever given a chance. Not that she would get it.

Then the thought occurred to her that by bringing him as her date, she would technically get the chance. Partially, at least.

Something stirred inside her. Something…hopeful.

Sure, he was Juliet's ex. But he was still Wes. He was a good guy. He would be her date for the long weekend in Mexico. And the best part, she wouldn't have to go to her seventh Delta Gam wedding alone. She wouldn't have to be the poor, pitiful sorority sister who was hopeless when it came to men.

Plus, she didn't have anyone else banging down her door, so…

As if reading her thoughts, he asked, "Do you have any other prospects right now?"

She traced the rim of her coffee cup with a finger. "No."

"Perfect, so there's no one to stand in my way. I can have you all to myself."

Her hand froze. A zing raced up her spine at that statement, which was ridiculous because he definitely didn't mean it in the context she took it. But hell, she wasn't going to worry about semantics right now.

"I'll take you with me to Mexico, and that's it?"

"That's as far as I've thought this through, yeah," he said. A pause, then as if impatient for her response, he asked in a rush, "So, will you do it?"

She glanced up and watched Misty tip her silver flask up to take a long swig of the liquor inside, then she made a gesture at Teegan, urging her on.

"I have one condition," Teegan said.

"Name it." His impatience transformed into eagerness.

"While we're at the wedding, you're there with me. You can have the rest of the weekend to do whatever you want. But any wedding events and the ceremony itself are mine. You stand by my side and act like a proper date, deal?"

There was a moment of silence and Teegan almost lost her nerve, calling the entire thing off.

Then, with satisfaction in his tone, he said, "Deal."

Chapter Two

This was going to be perfect.

Wes Stevenson approached the row of blue chairs at Gate B12, his eyes on nothing but Teegan. He'd coordinated to meet his sister, brother-in-law, and Teegan on the short connecting flight into Mexico so he could get Teegan to agree to the rest of his plan. He'd told her he was winging the trip, but that wasn't the whole truth. Not even close. If his scheming went the way he was hoping, Juliet would be eating out of the palm of his hand by the end of the weekend.

And then he would walk away from her just as easily as she had walked away from him. Right after ruining her wedding.

The grip on his carry-on bag tightened, his knuckles cracking from the strain. He was over Juliet, he'd been over her since the day her narrow waist and silky blond hair strolled out of that hospital room after his doctor's grim prognosis. If Wes couldn't play football anymore, and would lose his endorsement deals, then there wasn't room in her life for him. His back teeth locked down as he shook his head. He'd actually believed she'd loved him. As in forever and ever. For better or for worse. But she'd only loved his money and posh life, and he'd been too smitten to notice. *Idiot.*

Wes inhaled a few deep breaths, working hard to ease his racing pulse as he drew closer to the gate.

Like a beacon to his true north, he located Teegan immediately. It reminded him of college when he, Misty, Teegan, and Juliet had attended parties and formals together. There always seemed to be a warm, inviting light surrounding Teegan, pulling him in. *A ray of sunshine.* That's how he thought of her. He couldn't help but smile when she was near. If he and Juliet hadn't been seriously dating back then, he would've wanted to spend more exclusive time with Teegan.

Wes was excited at the prospect of getting his revenge on Juliet, and Teegan most definitely played a large part in that, but there was something more about the woman he was currently staring at. He liked her. He always had. Not just as Misty's friend, but as the bright spot in his messed-up world. The woman who seemed to be able to reset his compass with just a mere look his way. It's why Teegan was the only one he thought of for this whole charade. He couldn't—didn't want to—do this with anyone else.

She was sitting next to his sister at the gate, playing on her phone with one leg crossed over the other. She wore a yellow strapless sundress and flip-flops with a wide-brim straw hat resting in her lap, looking the picture of perfection for a beach wedding.

And the picture of perfection to make his plan work.

Her chin-length, wavy blond hair was swept up onto one side with a flower-shaped clip, drawing attention to her blue eyes and high cheekbones. What a welcome sight. It had been a few years since they'd seen each other—a previous Delta Gam wedding if he remembered correctly—and he felt a sense of ease at seeing her again.

Pulling off this arrangement with someone like Teegan would be a piece of cake. They knew each other. They liked each other. They shared mutual respect between them.

She must have sensed his approach because she looked up and met his gaze directly. A wide, unfiltered grin broke across her face, giving his stomach a small flip. His pulse picked up again, but this time it was into an excited trot, rather than a disgusted race.

Yeah. Getting his revenge wouldn't be a hardship at all.

"Wes," she said in a relieved tone. "You came."

Her words were simple and innocent, but it was the slight pitch in her voice that made him falter a step.

You came.

Had she been worried he wouldn't?

It was then that he realized how much she also had riding on their agreement.

Much like him, it was self-preservation.

"Of course I came," he said. "It's great to see you, Teegan."

"You too." Her cheeks filled with color as her gaze quickly dropped back to her phone.

An irritated grunt erupted next to Teegan.

"It's not nice to see us?" Misty turned to her husband. "You hear that, Jim? He hasn't seen his sister in months and has yet to acknowledge her presence. Goes right to Teegan first. I see how it is." She crossed her arms and gave her best attempt at a pout.

Smiling, he placed his bag on the ground and held his arms out wide.

Two seconds flat, and Misty was leaping out of her chair, throwing herself at him.

He arched his back, sweeping her short legs off the ground. Lowering his voice to a whisper, he hugged her tight and said, "It's good to see you, sis. I've missed you."

"Missed you, too, you big lug."

She held on a few minutes, so he let her have her fill, enjoying the ability to hold her in person rather than small pleasantries over the phone.

Pulling apart, he lowered her to the ground, and she patted his chest.

Jim stood in his salmon-colored polo shirt, khaki shorts, and leather shoes—his clothes exuding the Wall Street type he was. So different from Wes's comfy Under Armour T-shirt, shorts, and running shoes. Jim and Wes shook hands and exchanged greetings.

The three of them sat and look up at Wes expectantly, probably wondering why he didn't take his seat beside them.

Wes cleared his throat. "Teegan. Can I have a word?"

Misty narrowed her green eyes at him.

He shrugged like it was no big deal.

What he had to ask Teegan wasn't private. But he figured he'd get more accomplished without his sister's interference. If he and Teegan were going to do this, he wanted to make sure they were on the same page.

Teegan threw her phone into her bag on the chair next to her, then set the hat over it, and got up to follow him. He stopped in front of a large floor-to-ceiling window overlooking the small plane they were taking south.

"What's up?" she asked.

"It's about this weekend. I wanted to chat about how things are going to go down."

Her shoulders relaxed as she transferred most of her weight onto her right leg, cocking her hip out casually. "Sure. That's a great idea."

"As we agreed, you wanted a date for the wedding. And I was happy to step in. But, like I said, I have ulterior motives."

She nodded. "What Juliet did to you was terrible."

His stomach cramped slightly at her words, the reminder of his ex's betrayal still a sore spot. It likely would be until he exacted his revenge. Focusing on that impending satisfaction, he said, "I appreciate what you're doing. Letting me come with you to her wedding."

"Of course. I mean, the idea was a little weird at first. But I needed a date, so I'm glad it was…" She looked to the ceiling as if the right word was up there. She smiled at him. "Mutually beneficial."

"I did have—" He paused, trying to think of the right way to frame his next words. "Uh, there was something I wanted to run by you before we get there."

She straightened and gave him her full attention. "Anything."

Careful what you agree to.

His revenge knew no limits, so he'd need to remember to keep himself in check. He certainly didn't want to get a sweet woman like Teegan wrapped into crazy shit involving her Delta Gamma sisters only to regret it later.

But he needed to see how far she was willing to go.

He took a deep breath. "Teegan, how would you feel about us dating?"

Her light eyebrows shot into her hairline. "Excuse me?"

"For the wedding. What if we acted like we were together, as a couple? I mean, I'm your date, so people will probably assume anyway. What if we just played along?"

She blinked so rapidly he could barely see her eyes. "Played how? Like, touching? Hugging? K-kissing?"

"I don't think we'd have to show much PDA." He could've sworn he saw a flash of disappointment mixed with relief on her face before she shuttered the expression. "But I guess we can see how it goes. It might help drive the stake home when I tell Juliet about my secret."

He could picture it now. Damn, she was going to be pissed when she found out he was going to be playing ball again. Then he smiled, wondering how long it would take her to leave *this* fiancé.

"You want to act like we're a thing?" she said in a more composed voice. "To make Juliet jealous? In addition to telling her about the NFL thing?"

Making the biggest comeback in football history wasn't just a thing, but he let her comment slide.

"Yes," he said.

Her lips squeezed into a cute pucker as she nibbled on the inside of her cheek. "We'll act like a couple? Happy and stuff?"

"Yeah." Their fake bliss would be necessary to sell it to everyone.

She continued to watch him, a myriad of emotions soaring across her face. He was relieved to see the brief flash of nerves overshadowed by interest. "You'll dote on me and make me feel special?"

"Sure." It would be easy. Teegan had a heart of gold. It wouldn't be tough for people to believe he'd be attracted to a woman like her. She was honest and good to a fault. Which could be a problem. He didn't want to force her in too deep if she wasn't cool with it. He'd find another way to dig the knife into Juliet's wedding.

"Would you be okay lying to everyone?" he asked. "Just for the weekend?" Watching her expression, he didn't see anything that suggested she wouldn't do it. What he saw was curiosity.

Her lips twitched before they spread wide. "Everyone will think you're into me?"

"For this weekend, yeah."

"They'll think I finally found someone. That I'm no longer the Delta Gam who can't get dates. They'll think I snagged my best friend's hot brother."

"Yes." He stopped, then did a double take. "Wait, you think I'm hot?"

A blush rose from her neck and flooded her face. "Like you didn't know," she said as if that explained everything.

He noticed the looks he got from women. It wasn't hard to decipher their meaning. But something about the way she said it was different. So innocent and honest. Not to flatter or woo him, as other women had.

He cleared his throat, ignoring the stroke of heat filling his chest as he imagined Teegan saying other complimentary things to him. "Will you do it?" As he said the words, his body locked up in anticipation. He'd been waiting for the perfect setting to get back at Juliet. And this was another piece of that puzzle. He wanted it bad.

Her next words eased his tension and gave him a slight bit of optimism he hadn't felt in a long time.

"Hell yeah," she said. "Let's do this."

Her response was much more enthusiastic than he'd anticipated. She was, after all, Juliet's sorority sister and an invited guest at the wedding. But all right. Time to get down to business.

"What do we do now?" she asked. "Are we dating? Like right now? Or does the clock start when we get there?"

"We're not really dating, and we won't be after this weekend," he said quickly.

"Oh, right. Yeah. Of course." Embarrassment flew across her face, which made him immediately regret his comment. They weren't dating for real, but he didn't have to make it seem like an unfathomable notion.

Gentler, he said, "We can start when we get there, and we're around other people."

She was nodding as if taking mental notes.

"The more Juliet sees us together, the better."

"And what about our story? How and when did we start our relationship?"

"I don't think that's important. Just make something up. I'm most concerned about Juliet seeing us as a couple. Not how we got here."

Her expression glazed over in gleeful thought. "Okay. I can think of something."

He prepared for his next statement. This was the deal breaker. If she didn't agree to his next question, then their arrangement wouldn't work. They wouldn't sell it.

"Teegan," he started, trying to find the right words. It wasn't a big deal to him, but it might be to her. "How do you feel about sleeping with me?"

Her face drained of all color. "Uh...I...that's not necessary, is it?"

Shit. He was losing her.

"In the same room, I mean."

But, damn, the way the words stumbled out of her mouth stabbed him in the gut. Would being close to him be that bad?

"If we're going to make people believe we're a couple," he went on, "we should stay in the same room. Are you okay with that? Sharing a room with me?"

She swallowed, and her head nodded as if on a spring. "Ye-yeah. I mean, it makes sense, right?"

Why did she look like he'd said he was sending her to a maximum-security prison?

"Are we all good?" he asked. "Any other questions?"

"Th-the bed," she said, the words coming out rough. "When I booked, I got a single queen." Her gaze raked from his tall frame down to his shoes and back up. "Seems like a small bed for you. We'd have to squeeze together in order to fit. Our bodies touching and rubbing against each other." Her eyes widened slowly and she licked her lips, her attention still roaming his body.

He let her have her fill, enjoying the vision her comment conjured. He'd never thought about Teegan in a sexual way before, but glancing at her now, his thought most definitely had merit. Especially as her teeth sank into her plump, pink bottom lip and she let out a throaty moan.

Energy exploded in his lower stomach, a feeling of extreme yearning blinding him in an instant.

Whoa. Where had *that* come from? He shook himself to come back to the present.

Teegan sucked in a sharp breath as her cheeks reddened and she looked away. "Never mind. Ignore me. We'll, uh…we'll make it work."

That terrified expression of hers wouldn't relent. Christ, he didn't want to scar the woman.

He'd already called the resort and upgraded her original room to a presidential suite with a California king. First, because he wanted Juliet to see them in one of the nicer suites. But also because he wanted to treat Teegan. He'd wanted two kings, but one California was all that was available. He could request a rollaway, which would suck because of his size. Or he could sleep on the sofa in the other room. Whatever she preferred. Either way, he'd still get what he wanted—Juliet craving what she could no longer have.

"It won't be a problem," he assured her. "We won't have to be in bed together."

She toyed with her hands in front of her, not meeting his gaze.

"Teegan," he said. "Look at me."

Slowly, she lifted her eyes.

"Tell me you're okay with this."

"I...I'm fine. All good."

"Then why do you look like you're dreading every impending second with me?"

"No," she rushed to say. "It's not that. It's just..." Her lips bunched in thought. "I've never had a date to a wedding. I guess I'm stressing about how I should act. Despite what you said before, this is a big deal. I don't want to screw you."

That quick, his mind went to a completely different version of screwing. One that placed him and Teegan in bed together.

Maybe something showed in his expression, because she seemed to catch on to what she'd implied, and quickly said, "Up. I don't want to screw up. Screwing you would be..." She looked away and lowered her voice. "Screwing you would be like a dream." Teegan let out a high-pitched yip and whipped a look at him. "I mean—never mind."

Man, she was cute. So different from the overly seductive women who usually circled him. He liked it. Her like *her*.

"You'll be fine," he said, not wanting to embarrass her. "Just be yourself. And from time to time, look at me like you worship the ground I walk on." He smiled, waiting for her to catch onto his joke.

When she did, she responded with her own slow smile. "You are pretty great."

His expression dimmed immediately. She needed to stop saying that kind of stuff to him.

He wasn't great. Not right now.

"One more thing," he said, determined to stay on track.

"What is it?"

"I plan on telling Juliet my secret the night before her wedding. You probably don't want to be around for that."

Juliet would take her rage out on anyone within a five-mile radius. And she'd specifically aim for the woman who made it possible for Wes to attend the wedding in the first place. He didn't want Teegan wrapped up in that.

"Oh," she said with a look of calculation. "Okay. Sure. I can go somewhere else. Just let me know."

Instead of feeling light like he wanted to, he felt dread. Disappointment.

He'd fallen quite a bit since Juliet. He hoped that once he made the bride feel the way he'd felt since she walked out, that he'd find relief. He'd stop wishing, hoping, and most of all, he'd stop hurting.

• • •

After his conversation with Teegan, Wes went to the ticket counter, waiting for a middle-aged man to print the two boarding passes Wes had requested.

Wes upgraded Teegan's ticket to first class with his. It was the least he could do. The woman was doing him the ultimate favor.

As he'd been making the purchase, he'd had the slightest tinge of guilt for using Teegan this way. He'd never used anyone in his life, least of all a woman, but he was desperate. Fueled by only one purpose.

"What exactly is your plan?" his sister's voice asked at his side. "Go down there and throw the good china onto the floor? Cut up Juliet's wedding dress? Put itching powder in the groom's underwear?"

He liked the last idea a lot.

Wes glanced her way, touching his chin to his chest in order to look into her green eyes. He'd always been a big boy, coming in around six-five, two-eighty, but standing next to his five-foot-nothing sister, he looked like a giant.

The man behind the counter appeared with papers in his hand. "Here you go, sir."

Wes reached across, and as he took the boarding passes, the other man met his gaze. "Can I just say what a pity it was about your knee. Real shame. You were my son's favorite player. He's seven and wants to be just like you when he grows up. I don't have the heart to tell him he's got his dad's genes and won't amount to much size-wise, but he's determined. So I let it go. Nothin' wrong with dreaming a little, right? Even if it won't come true?"

That familiar stab of despair started to rise from his stomach, but this time it was washed out by Wes's new and improved reality. His knee was all healed, and he was ready to play again.

Letting the grin slide easily onto his face, he said to the man, "Thanks. What's your name?"

"Kevin."

"And your son's name?"

"Carter."

"Please tell Carter I said if he wants to play football, he can do it. Nothing can stop him if he sets his mind to it." Wes was living proof.

Kevin drew back, his eyes filling with delight. "Thank you, Mr. Stevenson. He's never going to believe I met you."

"You gotta phone?" he asked.

It took the man a second to catch on to Wes's meaning. When it dawned, he dug in his pants pocket and pulled out his cell.

"Do you mind?" Wes held a hand out for the man's device and gestured to the counter.

"Not at all."

Making his way around to where Kevin stood, he took the phone and held it up so both of them were in the picture. The other man's smile was broad and proud, making Wes's chest fill with something he hadn't felt in a long time. Hope.

When they were done, Kevin thanked him, and Wes returned the sentiment with a firm handshake.

He turned to head back to his seat, but his sister's direct stare stopped him.

She wasn't giving him a you're a moron for doing this *look, but a* you better know what you're doing *one.*

He did. He knew exactly what he was doing.

"What?" he asked.

"You know what."

He did, but he liked antagonizing his sister.

Wes crossed his arms and balanced his weight on his heels. "All I want is to see her face when I tell her I'm playing again. That's it."

"Think she'll piss her pants?" Misty asked.

"God, I fucking hope so."

Misty let out a chuckle. "In her fancy white wedding dress. Please. It has to be in the dress."

His sister and Juliet were sorority sisters and at one time real friends. Not like she and Teegan were, but they got along.

Until Juliet left him. People had to take sides, and of course, Misty was on his. His sister was invited to the wedding, probably out of courtesy. It was Juliet's big day; she'd want everyone there to witness it.

"This is just for the wedding, right?" Misty asked. "You and Teegan. When all is said and done, I don't want anyone getting hurt."

"Won't happen."

"You say that now, but I've already lost one friend over this shit."

"Friend?"

She leveled him with a look. "I liked Juliet. Don't love her like Teegan. But she was still a friend at one time."

"No one said you couldn't be her friend anymore."

She stared at him like she was ready to sock him in the chin. He rocked back a little just in case. "Who was there for you when Juliet walked out, and you were helpless in that hospital bed?"

"You."

She gave a sharp nod. "Damn right. A *friend* wouldn't do what she did."

"Then why the hell are you coming to her wedding?" he asked.

Misty scoffed. "This is vacation, buddy boy. Jim and I need this time to get his gentleman sausage and my lady bun to reconnect. We haven't had sex since—"

Wes threw his hands over his ears and started humming. "I don't want to hear it! I don't want to hear it!"

She threw her head back and chuckled.

When it looked like her mouth wasn't forming words and he thought the threat of her assault was over, he uncovered his ears.

"I'm just saying," she went on. "It's been tough at home lately. Juliet's invite was the perfect excuse to get away for a long weekend. Just the two of us. Plus, I want to see the other girls. It's been awhile since we've all been able to let loose."

"You and Jim okay?" he asked.

"Yeah, yeah," she brushed the comment aside. "We're solid. It's just...life, you know? It's not easy. Throw two kids in the mix, and it's even harder. This is our chance to work on us. Even if I have to fake happiness for one hour as Juliet walks down the aisle."

His stomach plummeted at the image his sister's comment conjured. His fists tightened, but he reminded himself that he was going to get the last laugh. As soon as he arrived in Mexico.

Wes glanced behind him at the rows of chairs outside the gate, scanning the crowd of people waiting to board. Teegan found his gaze and, on contact, she beamed at him. A full-watt smile that made his lungs squeeze. He wasn't doing anything different than what he'd done for her in college. They'd gone to events together before as friends, no big deal. But something about this felt different. Today she looked at him like he was her savior. And that was a status he'd long forgotten how to be. She needed a date, so he'd stepped in. Simple as that.

He wasn't here to save the day for anyone.

Chapter Three

They made it to Mexico with no issues. The flight was smooth, given the awesome treatment Teegan and Wes had received in first class. Mimosas, hot towels, and hell, she was half expecting a foot massage. She'd wished the flight had been longer so she could've taken advantage of the three-course meal the attendants talked about preparing.

Teegan had thanked Wes a bazillion times for upgrading them and had offered to pay the difference in cost. He refused, which she figured he would. It wasn't a secret to anyone that he was a millionaire; he could afford two first-class tickets. But she felt bad. He was helping her as much as she was helping him, so she wanted all transactions to be split evenly.

They'd arrived at the all-inclusive resort a little after one that afternoon, and immediately she wanted to relax. She had a hot date for the wedding. The sun was shining brightly. And their suite overlooked the secluded, white sandy beach. Their accommodations included a soaking tub, private wading pool, and balcony the size of her apartment back in New York. All thanks to Wes.

Wes.

How was she going to pull this off? Wes was hers this week. Hers.

Except he wasn't. There were rules—boundaries for their "relationship."

She wouldn't be able to relax one bit during this trip. Not when she imagined Wes sleeping in the same room with her. No shirt. Low-slung shorts like the ones he'd worn on the plane. It didn't take a genius to figure out what kind of yummy goodness was hiding under his clothing. If he'd been working out and getting into top physical shape for football, she could already picture his perfect physique.

That didn't settle her nerves at all.

And what about her role in this? The part she needed to play. If she didn't act the right way or say the right things, everyone would know they were faking a romance. The embarrassment for her would be acute, but nowhere near as bad as it would be for Wes. He'd lose his opportunity to confront Juliet and gain the closure he needed.

It was so much pressure.

She blew out a frustrated breath. Thank gosh he wasn't in the room. It gave her the extra time she needed to put her thoughts in order.

As soon as they'd checked in, he'd dropped his luggage and left. He said something about scoping out the resort and would be back for the welcome dinner later, but she knew the real reason. He was looking for Juliet. Part of her felt sad about their arrangement. Deep down, she'd hoped he'd come because he wanted to be there with her. Because of Teegan. But it wasn't. It was merely two people who needed something from the other. She couldn't deny the electricity that had passed through her as she'd entered the hotel with Wes, and everyone around them gawked openly.

After hanging her clothes in the closet and storing her rolling suitcase out of sight, she changed into her bathing suit, snatched a towel from the massive bathroom and left to meet one of her sorority sisters at the beach.

Saylor was one of the nicer Delta Gams. Not that the rest of them were awful, but Saylor had a way about her that was wholesome. She was the unicorn of women who never had a bad thing to say about anyone and always wore a smile—even had a sweet,

Southern accent. Apart from Misty, Saylor was one of Teegan's favorite sisters.

"Isn't this wonderful?" Saylor asked, stretching out on a lounge chair in her red and white polka dot bikini. Long, glossy blond hair spread around her like a halo; enormous black shades made her look like a movie star.

"Mmm." Teegan was in a state of bliss, lying facedown, enjoying the first kiss of sun on her ultra-white back.

"I hate how the only time any of us see each other is when someone gets married. It's been two years since Avery's wedding. That's too long."

Agreeing, Teegan adjusted on her chair, smoothing the soft cotton towel under her face. She closed her eyes. "Who do we have left? Maybe we can hurry them along."

Saylor didn't say anything for a few beats.

Lifting her head, Teegan shot a glance at her friend. "What?"

Saylor's lips were pulled in like she was trying to hold off whatever she wanted to say. "It's you," she finally said. "You're the last Delta Gam to get married."

Her stomach sank. "Oh, right. How could I forget?"

Saylor waved the comment away. "Don't you worry, sugar. We'll come up with something else, so you don't feel like it's all on you to get us back together. We've been talking about doing a girls' trip for a while," she went on, "I think it's time we stop talking and starting planning. We love you just the way you are. You don't need to rush to find someone on our account."

But it wouldn't hurt. The last few years, the getaways had been "couples" oriented. Teegan usually found out from Misty that an invite hadn't been sent to Teegan because of her single status.

Her sisters hadn't wanted her to feel left out, they'd said. Of course, not asking her at all solved that problem.

Teegan rested her cheek on the chair and looked at her sweet friend. "How's David? Did he get that promotion he was going for?"

"Yes, he got it," Saylor said. "I told him he would, but you know how he worries."

"Where is he? Not a *lie in the sun* kind of guy?"

"He went golfing with the rest of the husbands. Won't be back until later tonight. I'm glad he got the chance to go. He's been working so much lately. He hardly played last summer." She rolled onto her side with a hand under her head and shot Teegan a look. "So, you and Wes, huh?"

She didn't say it with her usual smile, but it wasn't like she was probing for gossip, either. She did seem surprised though.

Her sisters must think it odd that Teegan brought the bride's ex to the wedding. A pang of regret filled her. If roles were reversed and Juliet had brought Teegan's handsome, pro football player ex to her wedding, Teegan wouldn't be very happy.

"We just checked in," Teegan said. "How'd you hear already?"

One shoulder went up. "He's the talk of the resort. Grown men are salivating that the Texans Super Bowl MVP is here." She reached for the fruity umbrella drink on the table between them. After a quick sip, she said, "I don't remember hearing that you guys were together. How did it come about?"

"We're not," she said.

You're faking it, remember?

When Saylor's eyebrows furrowed, Teegan corrected, "It was really recent. We're not official, but I guess you could say we're dating. Went on dates. A few dates." No dates at all. Ever.

Shit. She didn't want to lie to her friend, but she also didn't want to say I brought him because I couldn't stand to watch all my beautiful sisters with their amazing husbands and feel jealous because I don't have—and might never have—the love that they do. Oh, and if that's not pathetic enough, Wes only agreed to come because he wants revenge on Juliet. Not because he wanted to be my date.

No, thanks.

"It's pretty serious," Teegan blurted out.

"What is?" Saylor said, looking at her with a puzzled expression.

"Me and Wes."

"I thought you just said it was new."

"It is. Was. It's new and it's old at the same time."

What was she saying?

Shut up right now!

Saylor's expression morphed from puzzled to full-on my friend needs her meds.

Teegan cleared her throat. "What I mean is, we haven't been official that long. But we've known each other for years, so that heightened our...love for each other."

"Love?" Saylor lifted her sunglasses to her forehead, looking directly at Teegan with widened vibrant blue eyes.

Love? Are you nuts?

Wes said to pretend you were dating, not in love!

Too late.

"Wow, Tee. I'm...wow." Saylor lowered the glasses to rest on her nose again and smiled in earnest. "Then I'm happy for you. I know you've been waiting a long time for someone special."

"Thanks," she mumbled as she relaxed back onto the chair, a fissure of worry coursing through her.

What the hell have I done?

Teegan propped her chin on folded arms and sighed, looking at the resort in the distance. "Do you think Juliet knows that he's my plus one?"

Probably hearing the worry in Teegan's voice, Saylor was silent another moment, then, "It'll be fine. She's getting married. I'm sure she's over whatever she and Wes had. No reason to worry."

Right. No reason at all.

Just life-altering humiliation if this all goes south.

• • •

Wes strolled along the beach, his flip-flops hanging from his fingertips, white T-shirt draped over one shoulder. He'd been touring the grounds of the five-star resort, thinking how this would've been his wedding.

A few months ago, that would've filled him with regret. Not anymore. He didn't want Juliet back. At least not in the waking hours, but he still felt…pissed about how things went down. Mostly because he wasn't what she'd wanted. He'd never been what she'd wanted. When she'd left, Juliet had made it clear that if he couldn't play football, then there wasn't a relationship for them. That was made even more apparent when she'd run into the arms of one of his teammates, LJ Young.

In hindsight, Wes probably should've seen the signs. How she lit up whenever he had a press tour to do. Or when he needed to make an appearance at some fancy fundraiser with Houston's elite. Or how she often talked to Andrew, his agent, about getting Wes additional sponsorship opportunities.

Yeah, the signs were there all along. He'd just ignored them. And that made him livid. He was so damn angry at himself for not pulling his head out of his lovesick ass to notice.

Wes cut up the beach at a faster pace, the pool area of the resort coming into view ahead of him, the suite his intended destination.

He was only wasting time. He hadn't located Juliet on his walk, and deep down he hadn't wanted to. Not yet. Nerves immediately kicked up, sending all sorts of thoughts through his mind. He imagined how happy Juliet and LJ were together, and he wondered what LJ had that he didn't. His stomach was a swarm of killer bees, the constant stinging a welcome punishment.

Needing to get his thoughts in order, he continued his ascent onto the patio of the pool, and through the back door toward the bank of gold elevators that led to the private suites.

Once inside his room, he heard rustling in the bathroom. Venturing in that direction, he found Teegan, wearing a black print bikini, her back to him, arranging bottles on the marble counter of the far sink.

"Have to line them up to see what I have," she said over her shoulder. "Hope that's okay."

He leaned into the doorway, crossing a bare foot over the other, watching her. They'd seen each other at summer parties in college where bathing suits were standard attire, but this was different. She had an air about her. A confidence. Juliet used to run and hide if he'd caught her looking anything other than what she thought was one hundred percent perfect.

Not Teegan. She stood there in that little bikini, minding her own business like he wasn't even there. And he found that he liked that. A lot. It was refreshing for a woman to be comfortable in her own skin.

"It's your side of the bathroom," he said. "Feel free to do what you want."

He couldn't remember Teegan looking so good in a bathing suit. Maybe he'd been blind in college, or she'd filled out since then, but the woman had curves in all the right places. Full, round ass that would take up his large hands. And breasts that spilled from the cups of her top, making him imagine kissing down the column of her neck and opening his mouth to—

What was he thinking? She was Misty's best friend and doing him a favor.

He was here for revenge. Not sex.

Though, revenge sex…

Never mind.

"Hey, there's something I have to talk to you—" She turned with a smile, then her gaze went directly to his bare chest, causing her face to fill with color. Her eyes glued to his pecs. Her mouth opened once like she wanted to say something, but then it closed. Opened. Closed. Something damn close to desire filled her expression, which did nothing to tear his thoughts away from revenge sex.

Without thinking, he stepped toward her.

Then a clear bottle dropped from her hand, slamming against the tile floor.

Glass shattered, sending shards flying.

Wes blinked, forcing himself back to the present.

Teegan shrieked and fell to her knees, hastily swiping pieces into a pile with her hands.

"Don't move, Teegan."

"I'm sorry. I'm so sorry!"

Why the hell was she apologizing? It was an accident.

"Stop moving, Teegan."

She continued to crawl across the tile, sliding glass into little bunches.

"Damn it, Teegan, stop!"

She listened that time, slowly lifting her eyes to his. "Sorry."

"Stop apologizing," he said. "And please stop moving. I don't want you to cut yourself. Just stay put a second. I'll be right back."

He walked out of the room and called the concierge for help. Like the attentive service one would expect from the high-end resort, staff appeared with brooms, vacuums, dustpans, and bags, cleaning up the danger within minutes.

After walking the team out, he came back and saw Teegan standing at the open balcony door, a breeze blowing her blond chin-length waves.

"You okay?" he asked. "You didn't cut yourself, did you?"

She didn't turn, but she did shake her head.

Seeming to need a moment, he waited.

It didn't take long before she faced him and let out a long, slow breath. "I have to tell you something."

"Sure, what's up?"

"I told Saylor we were dating."

"Okay," he said.

"I'm sorry."

Apologizing again. "For what? That was the plan."

She winced. "But I also told her we're in love."

Whoa. Okay, that was a little more than dating.

But, it *would* help his cause. If everyone at the wedding thought they were serious, then Juliet would think he'd moved on and he was happy. Yeah, happy and back in the NFL.

And completely unavailable to her.

The delight that came to him was fast and satisfying. Why hadn't he thought of that? Teegan was a genius.

"No problem," he said.

"No problem?" she asked. "Maybe you didn't hear me. I said I told Saylor—"

"I heard you just fine. I think it's great. We're in love. Let's celebrate."

Teegan looked at him like he'd suggested they go streaking through the hotel. "What if someone finds out?"

He shrugged, turning toward the mini fridge. "Let's hope they do."

"But..."

Bending, he pulled out a tiny bottle of red wine. "Look, anything I can do to get Juliet to see what she's missing, the better. If that means we put on a show like we're in love, then so be it."

"Are you feeling okay?"

"Perfect," he said, flashing her a grin. "Want a drink?"

She watched him for a few seconds, probably to see if he was going to lose his shit.

He might. Just not today.

"No, thank you," she finally said. "I'm, uh, going to take a shower and get ready for dinner."

"Suit yourself." Wes's plan was to drink this entire bottle of wine to calm his eager pulse. He lifted the bottle, squeezing one eye closed to get a better look.

Two or three more then.

Chapter Four

Teegan followed Wes's lively strides to the beach where candles and tiki torches illuminated three rows of rectangular tables covered in baby-pink organza and outlined by white Chiavari chairs.

You can do this. You can do this. You can do this.

She could pull this off. It was Wes for crying out loud. How many women would kill to be in her place right now? A bunch. She needed to pull herself together and put on a show.

She went for her most colorful and best-fitting outfit tonight, wanting the additional confidence. She'd worn it before and felt great in it, so she knew it would help her tonight. It was a wrap-around skort ensemble that had bright splashes of orange, pink, and yellow. The V-neck dipped just low enough to be risqué without being slutty, and sleeveless to show off her arms. The hem hit her at mid-thigh, and paired with her tan platforms, helped give the illusion of longer legs than she had.

It hadn't hurt when she'd walked out of the bathroom, Wes had grinned and his eyes glimmered as if satisfied with her choice.

His approval had been a dazzling sight. One she wouldn't mind seeing more regularly.

No. His approval doesn't matter. He needs something from you this weekend. He'd approve even if you wore an egg carton on your head and a brown sack as a dress.

As they drew closer to the dinner location, encountering more people, Wes slowed his pace. Instead of being a few steps ahead of her, he was walking at her side now.

She peeked a glance up at him, catching only a broad shoulder because of his height. His long arms swung at his sides, his posture rigid as he stared at the romantic beach scene in front of them.

They were about thirty feet from the other guests when Wes slipped his hand into hers.

She stiffened on contact and her brain shut off.

Low, so only she could hear, he said, "We have to sell it, remember?"

She nodded, not trusting herself to say anything while her heart did back handsprings in her rib cage. Holy crap. She was totally holding Wes Stevenson's hand.

And she *totally* sounded like a teeny bopper thinking that.

Be cool, Tee. Be cool.

It was going to be tough though since her version of cool had never been anything close to his. Or anyone else's for that matter.

Standing up straighter, she closed her hand around Wes's, enjoying the feel of his skin. The slightly roughened sensation beneath her fingertips sent additional sparks along her body, shocking it to awareness.

The closer they got to the already filled area, the more erratic her heartbeat became. She was going to face Juliet, her family, and friends. And they were all going to chastise and ridicule Teegan for bringing Wes.

Damn. She wished she'd thought about that before this moment. She could've feigned sickness for the entire weekend. What was going around right now? Yellow fever? Malaria? She'd even take a good case of salmonella. Anything to get her out of seeing the judgment in everyone's eyes. The same judgment she saw at every other Delta Gam wedding she'd attended.

With a date, without a date...it didn't matter. It followed Teegan anyway.

The man in question didn't seem bothered by their impending fate. He stood tall and wore a confident smile. Zero nerves radiated off him.

The Ice Box, they'd called him on the football field. Because he was always cool under pressure. Man, what she wouldn't give to have some of that superpower right now.

He squeezed her hand, causing her to look up at him. He lifted his chin, gesturing in front of them. She looked toward a receiving line that included the bride and groom.

Juliet and the man she'd left Wes for.

Excellent. Teegan couldn't wait to greet them both on this glorious, fantastic evening.

Why, oh why, had she agreed to this? It would've been better not to attend the wedding at all. And definitely not with Juliet's ex.

Oh, God. Her heart was beating at an unhealthy rate. She might faint.

Hey, that wasn't a bad idea. If she fainted—

The hand attached to hers tightened.

Wes. She was doing this for Wes. Just think about that. This had to be a million times worse for him.

Closing her eyes for a split second, she prepared herself.

There were two couples ahead of them, so she and Wes stopped and waited for the men and women to move along. Her pulse roared, and her body started to shake.

Be strong. This was difficult for him too.

Then it was their turn.

He glanced down at her through lowered lashes. *Ready?* his look said.

Teegan gave a slight nod. She could do this. She could talk to her college friend while holding the hand of said friend's smokin'-hot ex, while breathing, putting one foot in front of the other, and not passing out.

That would be *her* superpower.

Wes stopped them in front of LJ and Juliet.

"Wes," Juliet said with surprised eyes. She'd known he was here, of course. According to Saylor, everyone knew he was here. But the shock of seeing him was evident in Juliet's expression. She ran her gaze down his front from his short golden-brown hair, extra-wide chest, trim waist, and long, muscular legs, then back up. Juliet's shock morphed into something resembling a slow-burning flame. Low, but powerful. Dim, but unwavering. Something that couldn't be extinguished.

Wes caught it too, because he smirked knowingly as he said, "Hey, Jules."

Juliet blinked a few times, seeming confused by the sight in front of her.

You and me both, sister.

"LJ," Wes said, eyeing the man next to Juliet. His voice didn't hold contempt, but the greeting wasn't exactly pleasant, either.

And no wonder. LJ Young had been one of Wes's teammates. And would be again once everyone found out he was off the DL.

Aw, shit. This wasn't going to be good. Teegan glanced back and forth from one man to the other, expecting her heart to leap out of her chest and go sprinting down the beach in hysterics.

LJ was as tall as Wes, but not as broad. Which made sense since Wes played defensive end and LJ was a tight end. Wes was built for power, while LJ was built for speed and taking hits.

And what a pair LJ and Juliet made—both beautiful with blond hair and blue eyes. The all-American couple.

LJ's expression was cordial enough. Aloof, even. Which was too bad. The poor guy didn't even notice the muscle beating double time under Wes's left eye.

An awkward silence passed, then LJ stumbled forward as if Juliet shoved him toward Wes.

Teegan held her breath as the other man stretched out a hand.

"Wes, how ya doin'? It's been a while."

Wes's eyes dropped to the hand, then flicked them up to his face.

After another moment and a glance at Juliet, Wes's lips twitched. Then he smiled brightly. "Yeah, it has been a while. Things are good. Real good, actually. Thanks."

LJ was nodding, almost on automatic. "Good to see you up and about. The way the docs talked, I expected you to be on crutches for a long while." His gaze scanned Wes's body, the same assessing glint in his eyes that Juliet had. Teegan thought she saw a hint of disappointment in the other man's expression though.

"No crutches," Wes said. "In fact, I'm looking forward to swinging this beauty around the dance floor." He tilted his head toward Teegan, which prompted everyone else's attention to turn to her.

Dance? Shit. That wasn't part of their agreement. If anyone had two left feet, it was Teegan. She was not going to be responsible for putting his life—and his newly rehabilitated knee—in jeopardy.

But she was playing a part this weekend. Hopefully, the woman she chose to be the night of the wedding had some Ginger Rogers in her. Or Beyoncé. At this point, she'd take what she could get.

Teegan swallowed her swiftly rising anxiety, hoping like hell no one around could smell her fear. The corners of her lips went up but judging by the way Wes's jaw worked after she did it, it wasn't convincing.

She'd have to work on that.

"It's good to see you, Wes," Juliet said, her eyes plastered to him. "I have to admit that I was a bit taken aback when I heard the news about you two." She skated a look at Teegan, her implication clear.

Wes's date was the last person anyone expected.

Teegan didn't move. Her brain was using all its power to keep her body upright, and that was the best use of its time right now.

Wes must have sensed her discomfort because he released her hand to wrap a tight arm around her, pulling her against him. She wasn't even going to process how much she liked the way she fit into his armpit. Mostly because fitting into another person's *armpit* didn't sound like something one would revel in. Underarm? Lower shoulder? Upper oblique?

Her brain forgot about the holding her up part and the various vocabulary choices, and instead registered how much she liked being sandwiched against his warm frame. She melted into him, her arm instinctively wrapping itself around his waist.

Damn, his entire body was hard. And full of muscle. Just like she'd imagined.

Without being able to stop herself, she gave his side a good, sturdy squeeze, testing the firmness. Then she splayed her fingers wide, taking in more terrain, gliding her hand up and down his bubbly side.

Bubbly? Would we call it bubbly?

Well, it certainly wasn't smooth. It had bumps and ridges, each one harder than the next. The density was like the long tubes of bologna her father used to get at the meat counter back home.

Good Lord, Teegan. Really?

Yeah, because when one's arm was around a hot man, it was natural to think about deli meat.

No wonder you've been dateless for so long.

She nearly rolled her eyes and would have if Juliet hadn't been staring at her like she could read every one of Teegan's moronic thoughts.

"Juliet," Wes said in a purposeful tone. "You remember Teegan."

"Of course." She leaned forward to give Teegan a small hug. The kind that only required half an arm and a pat on the back. "It's nice to see you. With Wes, no less."

"Yeah, well…" Teegan glanced up at the tall, mountain of a man and tried to flutter her eyelashes. She must've done it too fast because her vision went wonky, causing her to sway a little and nearly lose her balance. Shifting her weight, she planted her feet firmly and looked back at Juliet. "We're in love."

Oh, geez.

Smooth? You call that smooth?

She could've sworn she heard a groan next to her, but she wasn't sure because Juliet's sharp intake of air drowned out just about every sound on the beach.

"Love?" Juliet's gaze zipped to Wes, searching for what seemed like confirmation.

There was a slight hesitation—hopefully Juliet didn't catch it—before Wes once again wrapped a tight arm around her. "What can I say? When you know, you know. It just kind of hit me…" He sent a cryptic look Teegan's way, and his jaw seemed to lock down. "Out of nowhere."

Teegan simulated an explosion with her hands, taking her fists and blasting her fingers open wide. "Boom."

Juliet glanced between them like she was waiting for one of them to admit this was a big joke.

When they didn't, Juliet tried to smile, but it was more like a light snarl with her top lip lifted above her teeth. "I'm so glad you both could make it. This is so…nice."

"It is, isn't it?" Teegan asked. "I was literally just thinking how nice this is going to be. You're going to be nice. I'm going to be nice. Everyone is going to be really nice this whole weekend. Especially to me. Let's make sure everyone is really nice to me."

Another groan sounded next to her, clear as day this time.

Juliet was giving her the *you missed your meds* look Saylor had given her earlier.

Shut up, Tee.

She squeezed her lips together as Wes thankfully dragged her away from the carnage her verbal diarrhea had caused.

• • •

What part of act normal and look at him in worship did she not understand?

Jesus, Teegan was killing him. Fine, she'd blurted out that they were in love. The surprise on Juliet's face was priceless. But he'd hoped to reveal everything a bit more strategically than that.

They reached the end of the farthest rectangular table to their assigned seats, and Wes pressed down on Teegan's shoulder for her to sit in the corner chair.

"I'm getting a drink," he said, his tone clipped. "Want one?"

"Please." The desperate plea in her voice made him pause and filled his stomach with guilt. He hadn't realized how much this weighed on her until she'd said that one word. No wonder she was a wreck in the receiving line.

Wes bent in front of her until their eyes were nearly eye level. He rested his hand on her thigh. Where her outfit ended, half his hand was on the material and the bottom half on her bare skin. "You doing okay?"

She nodded, but it looked like she was putting on a brave face for his benefit.

He smiled, trying to reassure her. "You're doing great."

"I'm sorry, Wes," she said, bringing sad eyes up to his. "I suck at this. I definitely wasn't the right woman for—"

"Stop it." Wes dipped his chin, not letting her glance away. "You're the perfect woman for this."

She drew back, surprised by his vehement tone.

He was shocked too. Though he shouldn't be. There wasn't anyone else he'd want to be here with. The only reason he wasn't freaking out was because he was here with Teegan. She made it easy for him to be himself. Something he hadn't felt in a long while.

"You don't have to lie to make me feel good," she said softly. "I won't blow your secret. I'll do whatever it takes to help you."

And what about him? Was he doing what she needed?

"I appreciate that," he said. "But we have an agreement, remember? I'm here for you too."

Her gaze went to his hand on her thigh. When she brought it back to his, her cheeks were bright red. "Thank you."

A few seconds passed in silence as the two of them stared at each other. And for the briefest moment, he forgot this was all a ploy. That Teegan was looking up at him because she really wanted him. That his hand on her was because he wanted it there. That he couldn't stand not touching what belonged to him. A few more seconds, and he watched as she swallowed hard, which brought him out of his reverie.

He stood. Without thinking much about it, he placed a kiss on her forehead. "I'll be right back, okay?"

The red on her face deepened, and she nodded with eyes that were unnaturally wide. "O-okay. Th-thank you."

Wes went to the bar, waiting in line behind a shorter man in a white shirt and linen pants. After the guy turned with a Corona and an orange drink with an umbrella, Wes stepped up to the bar and ordered a beer for himself and a fruity cocktail for Teegan.

With drinks in hand, Wes took a few steps toward the table, but a female voice stopped him.

"Wesley Stevenson." His name was said with relief, judgment, and a bit of marvel.

Wes shifted around toward the direction of the voice, meeting the aging gray eyes of Etta Royce—Juliet's grandmother—sitting at the table to his right.

The older woman was perched in her wheelchair, wearing a silver short-sleeved dress that matched almost identically to the silver strands of her short hair. She held a glass of clear liquid and ice.

"Ms. Etta," he said, approaching. "How are you?"

She grunted, sizing him up. "Surprised to see you here. Come to stop the wedding, eh?"

He let out a chuckle, trying to cover up the surprise of seeing her. "Nah, just doing a friend a—" Shit. "Er, I mean. I came with my girlfriend."

"Mmm-hmm," she said, her eyes taking on a knowing glint. "Pity."

"Pity?"

Her expression sharpened. "Oh, come now, Wesley. You mean to tell me you believe that those two are in love?" She slid a look at the bride and groom, who were still greeting their incoming guests.

He watched their body language, taking note of the non-cohesive way they moved. Not really in tandem. Just standing alongside one another.

Did that mean Juliet didn't actually love LJ?

Then why agree to marry him?

Juliet's gaze found Wes's, connecting immediately and warming even faster.

Something sparked deep in his chest. A longing. He'd been craving that look for so long. Fantasizing about it. And later, having nightmares about it.

Why now? Why give it to him after she'd walked out and made it clear she didn't want him?

"Think they'll go through with it?" Etta asked.

He ripped his attention from his ex, catching the devious tilt of the older woman's lips.

Wes shrugged. "Doesn't matter to me."

"Doesn't it?"

He scoffed. "Not one bit. I hope they're happy together."

She let out a half laugh, half grunt. "That boy's an idiot. And she's just as much of one for going through with marrying him. I give it less than a year."

What the—? Did she just say that? Juliet's own grandmother?

"He's an idiot," she said again. "Admit it."

Wes laughed, agreeing but not saying it out loud. He and LJ had been teammates, but that didn't mean they always got along.

Her eyes once again scaled his body. "Getting along well on that leg of yours, I see. Looks like you made a full recovery."

Out of habit, he glanced down at it, regretting the move as soon as he found the three-inch-long white scars from his incisions, staples, and stitches. So hideous. But the outcome had been worth it.

"Yeah. Doing great," he said.

She grinned like she knew something Wes didn't, or rather, maybe something he *did* know. "She's gonna be surprised as shit when she finds out."

He whipped a look her way.

One corner of Etta's mouth was quirked, and her eyes sparkled.

Someone from the hotel staff came by and gripped the handlebars of Etta's wheelchair. "Ready to take your seat?" he asked.

"Good to see you, Wesley." She pointed to a table a few feet away, then said to Wes, "This weekend just got a whole lot better if you ask me."

Wes made his way back to Teegan, thinking about what Juliet's grandmother had said. Why the fuck was Juliet marrying LJ if she didn't love him? Or if her family knew they weren't a good match?

No. It didn't matter to him; he was over her.

But it still made him wonder.

He placed Teegan's drink on the table in front of her. She snatched it up and brought it to her mouth like she'd been stranded in the desert for weeks.

"Whoa, take it easy," he said, sitting next to her at the end of the table. "We've got all night to get through."

"I know," she said, after a quick breather. "That's why I need this." And she dove back in.

When she put the glass on the table, it was empty.

Okay, then.

Wes stretched an arm over the back of Teegan's chair and looked out at the crowd of people. He'd estimate a little more than a hundred guests. And he knew almost all of them. He caught the stares, not settling on anyone in particular as his eyes grazed. All the expressions were similar—curiosity and worry seemed to take precedence. Except, Ms. Etta, who was still grinning like someone had spiked her water.

Juliet and LJ finished greeting their guests and made their way toward the head of the first table. Having done the seating chart, she obviously knew where Wes and Teegan were sitting. She glanced out over the tables and found Wes's gaze immediately. Her expression heated with desire.

She could send all the come-hither looks she wanted. It wouldn't work. He'd come to Mexico for revenge, and that's what he was going to get.

Moving his chair closer to Teegan's, he put his arm around her. She seemed to like when he did it earlier. This time, she stiffened, which was something they'd have to work on.

Lowering his mouth to her ear, he used his nose to nudge some blond hair out of the way, and he whispered, "We have people watching."

"O-okay," she said just as soft, her body still strung tight. "What do you want me to do?"

"Play along." Then he touched his lips below her ear.

If he thought she locked up on him before, she was like Fort Knox now.

"Teegan," he said. "Relax. As far as everyone else is concerned, this isn't the first time I've touched you."

After a second, she released a long, slow breath. "Right. Sorry. You just surprised me. I'm ready now."

He smiled against her skin, noticing faint traces of vanilla and lavender. He recognized the scent from the bathroom in their suite after she'd taken a shower. It was pleasant. He might've spent a few extra minutes during his own shower until the scent faded.

Placing their hands together, he kissed the top of hers, making her gasp.

Through a chuckle, he whispered, "Thought you said you were ready?"

"I…I am. I'm good. Do it again."

Keeping his gaze fixed on hers, he brought their joined hands up to his mouth and repeated the gesture.

"Oh, God," she hissed. "You can't look at me like that when you do it!"

"Like what?" he said, enjoying the hell out of her reaction. "This?" Feeling Juliet's gaze on them, adding fuel to his actions, he increased the heat in his eyes as he lifted their hands again. But this time, instead of kissing the top as Teegan expected, he flipped her hand the other way and flicked his tongue out to touch the inside of her wrist.

She let out a strained mumble of words he didn't catch. Then, "I'm trying. Jesus, I'm trying, I swear."

He looked at Juliet, who was watching, her lips twisted in a disgusted sneer. He brought his attention back to Teegan, and said, "You're doing just fine."

• • •

What happened to we shouldn't have to show PDA?

He should've warned her about what he was going to do. Given her a play-by-play. Isn't that what those sports guys did? Went over every move before executing? Lips touching her body parts required preparation. Lots and lots of preparation.

And his eyes. The way he stared at her with those sexy bedroom eyes nearly made her knees give out. Thankfully, she was in a chair. Passing out was one thing, but passing out while a man's mouth was on her would've been mortifying.

"Teegan, relax," he said again.

"I'm trying to," she said. "It's just…"

"Just what?"

Yeah, just what? You're a grown woman, about to have a panic attack because a man is kissing your hand and wrist. What are you going to do if a man kisses your mouth or…other places?

But this wasn't just any man. This was Wes. Something told her if another man touched her right now, it wouldn't be nearly as crippling.

He stopped, taking his lips away, but still holding her hand, and stared at her.

"It's…it's you," she said.

The sexy expression he'd been sporting dropped, so did his hold on her hand.

Crap. "Did I say something wrong?"

He shook his head, but she got the sense it was more to clear his thoughts. "No. You're good. It just surprised me, that's all."

Join the club.

He glanced up, and Teegan followed his gaze. Juliet was looking at them, and when she saw Teegan, she immediately turned her head to her fiancé.

And the realization hit.

People are watching.

Not people. Person. Juliet.

Part of their agreement—part of Wes's plan to make Juliet jealous. Touching and kissing another woman would certainly do that.

Why that gave Teegan an icky feeling in the pit of her stomach, she wasn't sure. But it did. She needed to get a handle on herself. Wes was doing this because of Juliet, not because he *wanted* to touch Teegan.

But that didn't mean she couldn't enjoy his touches and kisses. Even if it was short-lived and a lie. His touch sent shivers through her body, and she wanted to relive that sensation over and over before this weekend ended.

She snaked an arm inside the crook of his elbow, locking their hands, and she tipped her head on his shoulder. It was a firm, bumpy, yet comfortable pillow. She inhaled deeply and then exhaled the tension she'd been holding onto. Wes was hers for the next three days, and she was going to live it up.

It was Wes's turn to stiffen, but only for a second. Then he squeezed her hand, bringing it across his lap to rest on his large thigh. His thumb traced circles on the back of her hand.

"Well, well, well," a male voice said in front of them.

Teegan glanced up and met the dazzling smile of a man with mocha skin and welcoming brown eyes. He was standing, which prompted Wes to get to his feet. The man stretched an arm out, so Wes let go of Teegan to give the other man a hug with a fist to the back.

"Jamal," Wes said. "Good to see you, man."

Lowering into his seat across from them, the other man glanced between Teegan and Wes.

"This is Teegan," Wes said. "Teegan, this is Jamal Jenkins, Houston's star cornerback."

Jamal held out a hand, and when Teegan offered hers, he turned it over and kissed the top. "Nice to meet you."

Teegan giggled because it was so cute and old-fashioned, but it didn't do anything to her insides like when Wes did that move.

"Cornerback, huh?" she asked. "So that means you're pretty fast."

She knew enough about football from her dad, and then from watching Wes play in college and the pros.

Jamal's eyebrows lifted while Wes let out a laugh.

"I like your girl already," Jamal said. He turned to Teegan. "Yeah, I'm fast. Ask me about my time for the forty."

Still laughing, Wes said, "Knew that was coming."

"The what?" she asked.

"The forty-yard dash," Wes said. "It's something they clock when you're trying out for the NFL. Guys like Jamal get off on it because they can set records based on how fast they run it."

"You didn't have to run it?" she asked Wes.

Jamal threw his head back and cackled. Then he bent forward with his head between his legs, seeming to struggle with breath.

"Yes," Wes said. "I ran it. It's a requirement for everyone."

"And?" she asked. "How'd you do?"

Jamal got a handle on himself and lounged in his chair, grinning with a full set of pearly whites. "Some of us were built for speed, Teegan. Others…" His gaze raked over Wes. "Others were built to push three-hundred-pound meatheads away from the quarterback."

Wes slid a glance at Teegan. "Jamal thinks this is hilarious because he holds a record in the forty. And he doesn't let anyone forget it."

"Really?" she asked. "That's awesome. What record?"

He sat up straighter, adjusting the collar of his white linen shirt. "One of the top ten times in the forty-yard dash ever recorded."

"No shit?" she asked.

That earned an even brighter smile from Jamal, and twinkling eyes. "No shit."

She propped her chin on her fist and leaned over it toward him. "What was your time?"

He sat up straighter, the crisp white dress shirt showing off his lean, but muscular shoulders. "Four point three seconds flat."

Four and a half seconds? Dayum. "That's, like, faster than a car."

Jamal's face blew up like fireworks. "Now, I *really* like your girl."

Wes was shaking his head. "Please don't inflate his ego any more than it already is."

After the laughter had died down, Jamal looked at Wes. "How are you really doing? Things okay with you?"

Wes shrugged, which Teegan began to notice was his canned response when he didn't want to answer with the truth. Though, this time the truth was a good thing, so she didn't know why he didn't want to tell his friend what was going on.

Maybe because he wanted it to be a surprise for everyone. Not just Juliet.

"Things are good," he said. "Seriously."

"Well, you're up and moving," Jamal said. "You've got a beautiful, smart woman by your side. I'd say you're doing better than good."

Wes turned to her, coasting his hand down her thigh in a possessive way she found she liked. He gripped her leg above the knee.

She placed a hand on top of his. Their gazes connected, and something happened. It was weird. In a good way. His eyes softened, and a layer of brick he'd built up seemed to fade away. She felt something low in her belly that yearned for more of those walls to come down. For her to be the cause of them falling.

"Yeah." Jamal chuckled. "I think you're doing just fine."

A plate of colorful lettuce with tomatoes and cucumbers was placed in front of Teegan and then Wes, which broke their connection. Wes looked away, bringing his hands up to the table. She felt the loss of his touch immediately. Instead of hoping for something that could never be, she focused on the food in front of her.

Jamal cut through his salad. "When I heard you were here, I didn't believe it. I give you credit. Not sure my man sack is big enough to come to my ex's wedding."

Wes opened his light-pink napkin, held it up and shook his head, then placed the napkin in his lap. "Yeah, kinda crazy how it played out. Teegan and Juliet are sorority sisters. You remember Misty, right? My sister?" When Jamal nodded, he said, "They're all friends."

"Damn," Jamal said. "Small world."

"Claustrophobic." Wes drank from his beer. Setting it back on the table, he said, "I'm sucking it up for Teegan. These are her friends. I didn't want her to miss it because of me."

Jamal's eyes took on an assessing gaze. "That's it, huh?"

"Yeah," Wes said, keeping his eyes on his plate.

Jamal tipped his drink back. After a long swallow, his eyes took on a devious glint. "Aren't you just a good boyfriend."

"He is," Teegan said. She tried the eye flutter thing again, and this time she must have succeeded because Wes winked at her like he was satisfied.

Chapter Five

Dinner ended, and everyone got up from their table to either turn in for the night or mingle by the bar.

Wes meandered to the latter with his teammates. It was quite a view. Seeing them playing on TV was one thing. But having them standing together in regular clothes, all big and buff, was something else entirely. All of them were well over six-three and as wide as barns. Even Jamal, who was tall and lean, still looked as imposing as the rest. Like a group of Greek gods at social hour.

Teegan found her way to a group of her sorority sisters who were holding up the other side of the bar with drinks in varying colors.

Right about now, she could use a drink in every color.

As she approached, Avery, Jessica, and Saylor grinned at her, practically bouncing in place.

"Oh my God, Tee, I want to hear all about you and Wes!" Avery with her long brunette hair, rich brown eyes, and heart-shaped face wore an anticipatory expression that filled Teegan with excitement.

Teegan wasn't used to the attention. And frankly, she was enjoying it. She was accustomed to being the Delta Gam who rode the coattails of the other women, living vicariously through them when it came to men and relationships.

This was for her. Just this once they'd see her as their equal.

"Saylor said you're in love! Tell us everything."

Wes said he didn't care how they got together. That she could make something up.

Well, here it goes!

Teegan leaned in like she was telling her sisters a deep, dark secret. "He admitted that he always kind of wanted me, even while he was with Juliet."

"No," Jessica said through a delighted gasp. She flipped a long black section of hair over her shoulder. Jessica was the beauty of their small circle. Tall and thin, she was more Victoria's Secret model than average woman. Where most women had to work to look amazing, for Jessica it was effortless. "Now that I think about it, when we were in college, he did dance with you more than any other Delta. Probably more than even Juliet."

Saylor spoke next. "You're still in New York, right? And he's in Houston? How do you guys make it work?"

Teegan gave herself a few seconds to come up with a good answer. "He flies up all the time. He said he couldn't stand being away from me for too long. Plus, there's video chat and the phone. We talk constantly."

Avery sighed. "That's so romantic."

"He really is," Teegan said.

Or she imagined he was. She painted him as a romantic. His kisses were sure as hell romantic.

"How did you two get together?" Jessica asked. "Saylor said it was recent."

"Recent-ish," Teegan said. "Longer than people might realize. I went to Houston with Misty while Wes was in therapy. I wanted to offer support where I could."

Jessica's lush red lips spread wide. "Support how? Like sponge baths?"

"Yeah," Teegan said, feeling bold for the first time since she couldn't remember when. "And...other stuff." She let her tone imply additional naughty things.

Three mouths fell open.

"Teegan! You little minx!"

She shrugged like it was no big deal. But she was pretty sure she would've dropped dead if she'd seen or touched anywhere close to Wes's—*ahem*—man parts. She wasn't a prude, but it was Wes. Her version of male perfection. Her statue of David. Except with arms. Nice, big, strong arms that—

"So this was after Juliet had walked out, right?" Avery asked.

"Oh, yeah," Teegan said. "I never would've made a move on a sister's man."

"Of course not," they agreed with a nod.

Jessica glanced to her right, toward the opposite end of the bar where Wes stood, chatting with an equally tall guy with almost as many muscles. The other man's chest wasn't as big. Pity for him.

"He's looking good," Jess said. "I thought Juliet said he wasn't going to be able to do much after his injury."

"He's doing awesome," Teegan said. "Getting around really well. In fact, he's—"

Don't say it. Don't give away his secret.

Teegan squeezed her lips closed.

"He's what?" Saylor asked.

"Getting around really good," she repeated.

Jessica narrowed her eyes like she was trying to read Teegan's mind. "I think that's code for he's an animal in bed and his injury hasn't slowed him down one bit."

Saylor smacked Jessica on the shoulder as Avery laughed.

"What?" Jessica said. "I've heard stories about people having surgery and coming back even stronger. Wes is more powerful now, isn't he?"

Teegan's cheeks flamed hot, but she did her best to act casual and nod.

"I've been dying for Ian to break something," Jess went on. "Anything."

The ladies all laughed at the ridiculous statement about Jessica's ultra conservative accountant husband.

Avery finished her drink and placed the empty glass on the bar in front of them. "He must honestly care about you if he came to his ex's wedding so that you didn't have to come alone. I mean, I heard the breakup wasn't exactly amicable."

Hillary Kincaid and Samara Lee, two additional Delta Gammas approached, wearing matching sneers pointed at Teegan. The way the women glided across the sand in their skyscraper espadrilles and short, slim-fitting dresses was something to admire. Teegan would've broken an ankle and flashed everyone in the process.

"I think it's ridiculous that she brought him, don't you, Samara?" Hillary stopped in front of the trio with a hand on her narrow hip.

"Completely tasteless," Samara agreed. Her vibrant blue gaze cut Teegan up one side and down the other. "You used to be so nice, Tee. What happened?"

"Come on, girls," Jessica said. "Take it easy on her. She—"

"Is selfish for bringing him," Hillary cut in. "Can't she see what it's doing to Juliet?"

Everyone swung a look at the bride, who was at the bar laughing with her fiancé and some of his teammates.

"Yeah," Jessica said with a sardonic expression. "She looks torn up."

"She is," Samara said. "She's putting on a brave face for her guests."

"What's the matter with you?" Hillary looked with distaste at Teegan. "How could you think bringing him would be okay?"

"Th-they broke up and she's getting married." Teegan's voice shook.

Hillary crossed her arms over her ample size D chest. "That's your defense?"

Jessica stepped forward, half shielding Teegan. "What's your problem, Hill?"

"She's my problem." She pointed at Teegan. "After going to how many weddings dateless, she had to come to this one with the bride's ex? How desperate do you have to be?"

"Desperation had nothing to do with it," Avery said in Teegan's defense.

"Absolutely not," Saylor said in her sweet Southern accent. "They're in love."

"Love?" Hillary choked on the word.

Samara shook her head in disgust. "Coming with no date at all would've been better than disrespecting the bride at her beautiful wedding."

"I...I—"

Hillary sliced her hand through the air, dismissing whatever she wanted to say. "Have nothing to justify what you did."

She shifted to find Samara pinching her lips together. "Pathetic."

Then the two spun on their heels and walked away as if Teegan was a piece of garbage left out in the sun too long. Which was exactly what the women succeeded in making her feel like.

"Do you girls think it's weird?" Teegan asked Saylor, Avery, and Jessica. "That I brought him?"

"Oh, please," Saylor said. "You shouldn't put your life on hold because someone else might not like it."

Teegan rubbed away the tension headache that was seconds from starting. "I know. But it's still kind of shitty, right? Wes and Juliet shared a life together."

"And she walked out on him," Jessica said. "That was her choice. One she can regret for eternity now that he's moved on with someone else."

Teegan couldn't meet any of their eyes. "I still feel bad."

"Don't," Saylor said. "Juliet is getting married. Wes isn't hers anymore."

He wasn't Teegan's, either.

"How ya bitches doin'?" Misty said behind them, cutting through the gray haze of self-doubt Teegan was under.

A squeal sounded that nearly burst her eardrums. Everyone was exchanging hugs in an instant.

"What's with the gloomy faces?" Misty asked. Her auburn hair was a bit tamer tonight. The usually unruly waves were strategically placed to look textured rather than wild.

Avery frowned. "Teegan thinks everyone is mad at her for bringing Wes as her date."

Misty's features scrunched into a devil-may-care expression. "Fuck them. Juliet left him. It's her loss."

"That's what I said," Jessica agreed.

Misty called the bartender over for another round. "It's nothing that more drinks can't fix."

"Where have you been?" Jessica asked Misty, sliding her empty glass to the back of the bar. "We didn't see you at dinner."

"Jim and I were catching up on episodes of *The Walking Dead*."

Confusion passed over all three faces, no doubt wondering why a TV show outranked their friend's wedding, so Teegan said, "That was code for they were bumping uglies."

Misty grinned. "We were way behind. Needed at least three episodes to get caught up."

"Nice!" Jessica gave Misty a high five.

"Speaking of getting some," Avery said. "Tee was just telling us about her love affair with your hot-ass big brother."

Misty turned a baffled expression to Teegan. "She was?"

Shit. Shit. Shit. Teegan hadn't filled Misty in on the latest fake-relationship development. The *in love* part of it.

"Yeah," Teegan said through a chuckle she had to force out. "How Wes and I got together."

"And they're in *looooove*," Avery said.

Still staring at Teegan, Misty's eyes narrowed and lips gathered. "Love."

Damn it. Misty was only cool with the idea of Teegan dating Wes because she believed the whole thing was a farce. If she thought Teegan was going around telling people she was in love with Wes, Misty would put a stop to the charade pronto. Misty wasn't okay with any of her friends dating her brother in earnest, not even Teegan.

Teegan pleaded silently with Misty. Don't blow it. Please don't blow it.

Jessica pointed a deep-purple painted nail at Teegan. "I want the rest of the details."

"That's it," Teegan said, her imagination immediately squashed in Misty's presence. "I went down and visited him in Houston. And we started talking and seeing each other after that."

Avery gave Teegan a big squeeze and spoke into her ear. "I'm so happy for you, Tee. Honestly. You deserve this."

Her heart almost burst at those words. How long had she wanted to hear something like that from her friends?

Too bad the encouragement wasn't because of something real.

"Thank you," she said without much *oomph* behind the words.

When they pulled apart, Teegan caught the judgment in Misty's expression.

Crap. She had some explaining to do.

• • •

By the time Teegan and Wes made it back to the suite, both their asses were dragging. It had been a long day of traveling, eating, talking, drinking, and playing a part.

Who knew lying could be so exhausting?

They still had a few more days of it, so it was time to rest up and start again tomorrow. Something told Wes they'd need all the rest they could get if they were going to survive.

"I'm sorry again about today." Teegan kicked off her shoes by the closet. "Sometimes my mouth runs away from me. It just...I don't know. It felt good to *feel good* for a bit. The girls were doting on me and asking questions, and I wasn't used to it. I liked it." She sighed deeply. "I'll be better tomorrow. I promise."

Wes placed his hands on her shoulders and whirled her around to face him. "First, stop apologizing. I asked you to bring me, and I knew it wasn't going to be easy. You're doing great given the circumstances."

"Yeah, but now Misty's pissed at me."

"She'll get over it."

Teegan bought her dejected eyes up to his, making his chest ache. "She will. But it still sucks that she's mad to begin with."

"I'll talk to her," he said. "Get her to understand what's going on. She's pissed because she thinks someone is going to get hurt. I told her that's not going to happen. You and I both know what we're in for. It's just this weekend. It's not like we're going to date for real after this."

Teegan was nodding, but it seemed like her thoughts were elsewhere.

He dipped his head to meet her gaze. "We're good, right? We're both on the same page?"

"Yeah," she said, her gaze dropping. "We're fine."

Pressing her chin up to force her attention on him, he said, "Teegan, talk to me. What's wrong?"

"It's nothing. I'm fine."

"That's the second time you've used that word, so I know you're not. What's up?"

She waited a few moments, chewing on the inside of her cheek, before saying, "Tonight was rough."

"You can say that again."

"The disgust in Hillary and Samara's eyes when they told me I was pathetic was hurtful."

He froze. "What did you say?"

"Hillary and Samara," she said. "They told me I should've known better than to bring you as my date. That I was desperate for doing it." She glanced away, but not before he saw her lip tremble.

Damn them. He'd never liked those two. Troublemakers of the first degree.

Wes stepped forward so that he was in front of her, his chest inches from touching her nose due to his height. "I'm sorry."

Keeping her eyes diverted, she lifted her shoulders and mumbled something.

"Teegan, look at me."

When she slowly met his gaze, he repeated, "I'm sorry. They shouldn't have said that."

"Why? It's true. I am pathetic. I had to get my best friend's brother to come as my date, and he only agreed because he has beef with the bride."

When she put it that way, he felt like the worst sort of cad.

"Teegan, you know that's not the whole story."

Blue eyes stared back at him so miserable it almost tore him in two. "Really? Are you telling me you agreed to come for some other reason? Something that has to do with your feelings for me?"

"No, I just—"

"You only wanted to come because of Juliet."

"Yeah, but—"

"But nothing," she said. "This entire arrangement sucks."

"I know. But it's only temporary. We just have to survive for another few days."

"That's what sucks about it," she said.

"What?"

"Us. You and me. It's temporary."

Was she—? She couldn't be saying...

He stepped back. "Teegan, we can't. This wouldn't work after the wedding." Not that the idea of them together was so baffling, it just wasn't in the plan. He didn't want to move on with anyone else. He was still torn up about what happened with his last relationship. He was in no condition to do that again. And even if he wanted to, she was in New York. He was in Houston. Long distance never worked.

Her shoulders dropped. "I know. I didn't mean you specifically. But *someone* would be nice. Everyone is so happy for me. They keep congratulating me on snagging a guy as great as you."

As great as you. Why did it make him feel awkward every time she said that? Like he didn't deserve such praise. Especially from someone as good as her.

"It's not real," she went on. "And I want it to be. I want what my sisters have. What Misty and Jim have. And now that I've seen what it's like, even though it's fake, I want more. I want something real." She closed her eyes for a second as a flash of pain drifted over her face. When she looked back at him, she said, "Hillary and Samara were right. I did this because I was desperate."

He moved toward her and cupped her cheek, and she leaned into it. "I'm sorry, Teegan. I didn't—I should've thought about how this would affect you. I forced you into this without giving your feelings a second thought."

"You couldn't have known. You're used to having someone. You don't know what it's like to have your friends tiptoe around or exclude you from things because they're afraid of hurting you."

Actually, he did. After his accident, Jamal was the only teammate who visited or checked on him. Everyone else had left him to rot in that hospital bed. They'd had team parties, and he'd found out about them afterward through pictures in magazines. Not that he craved to go to those types of events, it was the fact that he'd been left out. Like he was no longer useful because of his busted knee.

He ran his thumb over her cheek, feeling the smooth skin. "I understand more than you know."

She seemed to try to smile, one side of her mouth went up, but it didn't go all the way or meet her eyes.

She didn't believe him. She thought he was placating her.

He glanced down at her lips, instantly wanting to kiss away that sad expression. Which was lunacy, because she was his sister's best friend and she'd been nothing but a friend to Wes. She was Teegan. Sweet, thoughtful Teegan. Who everyone loved, but never remembered to include in anything.

Sweet. Yeah, she was sweet. Sweet to touch and probably sweeter to kiss.

He lowered his head to do just that.

Her eyes widened, and a look of fear blasted across her face. She held her breath.

Wes stopped.

What was he doing? This was a surefire way to ruin their perfectly laid-out arrangement. This would complicate things. Not to mention it would royally piss off Misty. Plus, Juliet wasn't around, so what was the point?

Right. There wasn't any. The only reason he should want to kiss Teegan would be so Juliet could see it.

Not because he wanted to kiss her.

And he had wanted to kiss her.

She pulled away and didn't say anything as she went to the dresser where she took out a tank top and a pair of shorts. She carried them into the bathroom and shut the door, leaving Wes to wonder what the hell was going on.

He stared after her for about a minute before he got his brain on track. He readied his makeshift bed on the sofa in the other room—blankets, pillows, and sheets—stripped off his pants and shirt, and crawled under the blanket. Tomorrow was another day of this craziness.

Chapter Six

As was his routine the last few months, as soon as the sun rose, Wes was out of bed and dressed in his workout clothes.

He'd tried to be quiet as he got dressed, but it didn't matter. Teegan slept like the dead with covers pulled up over her head, and a soft, raspy snore coming out of her. It was cute for about two seconds until he realized he was standing at the side of the bed watching, thinking she was cute. That's when he'd snatched his running shoes and carried them out the door, slipping them on as he hustled down the hallway.

He and Jamal had agreed to meet at the hotel gym, and he was excited at the prospect of working out with someone other than himself for a change.

Until Jamal started to play shrink.

"You think this little honey of yours is the one, or what?"

Wes placed his back on the weight bench, beneath the bar, waiting as Jamal added the last fifty-pound weight on the end.

"Or what," Wes said, leaving it at that. He readied his hands, spreading them around the metal bar, and concentrated on his breathing.

"I don't know, man. You two looked pretty cozy last night."

They'd had to. For Juliet's benefit.

It didn't matter that warmth passed over him as he'd held

Teegan's hand in his. That he'd felt possessive over Jamal kissing the top of her hand. That when she'd placed her head on his shoulder, he'd almost sighed like a goddamn pansy.

It didn't matter. Because that's not what this was. It wasn't about finding someone else to fill his void. It was about revenge.

Once the weight was in place, Jamal stood next to the bar, placing his palm underneath to spot Wes.

"You know what your problem is?"

Wes lifted the bar off the holder and groaned. Not because of the additional weight he'd told Jamal to add, but because of his friend's invasive question.

"Do we have to do this right now?"

"Yeah, we do," Jamal said. "Remember who was there for you when you were stuck in that hospital bed. Remember who had to listen to you bitch and moan about how piss poor your life was because of your busted-ass knee. Remember who pushed you harder so you could heal faster and get back on the field."

Wes lowered the bar to his chest, then on an exhale, he pressed it upward. "Shit, man. You sound like my sister."

Jamal snorted. "At least someone has some sense."

"You didn't have to," Wes said, the words coming out strained as he repeated his rep. "Stay with me. I didn't beg you to, you asshole."

Jamal's bald black head came into view over him. "It's worse than I thought. This girl has you all up in knots."

"What?" The bar wobbled, tipping to the right a bit. Wes's hands squeezed the shit out of the metal in an attempt to not drop all 400 pounds onto the floor. With effort and Jamal's help, Wes righted the bar parallel to his chest. "I'm not in any knots. As a matter of fact, I'm completely knot free."

"Just you saying that tells me you're lying." Jamal faded from his view, but his hand remained on the bar for support. And he kept talking. "You don't know who you are without Juliet. That's the issue. And you're scared to find out. She used you up good, made you feel like nothing, and now you believe you are nothing. That without football, your life doesn't hold meaning."

Wes concentrated on his last few reps. It was difficult when every few seconds he'd get a flash of a cute blonde with a killer smile and peppy personality.

"And that's bullshit, man," Jamal went on. "Just because she couldn't stick around through the good and bad, doesn't mean Teegan won't."

Wes grunted as he threw the bar into the holder and bolted upright. "Why are we having this conversation?"

"Because you need to hear it."

"You've got a different woman every night. What do you care if I settle down with one?"

"Because I'm happy," Jamal said, dropping onto the bench beside Wes's.

"So am I."

"Yeah?"

"Yeah."

"Then why did you beg that girl to bring you to this wedding so you could get back at Juliet?"

Son of a—

He was going to kill his sister.

Wes leveled his friend with a look. "When did she tell you?"

"Last night," Jamal said. "Misty thought I might be able to talk some sense into your stupid ass."

"Sense about what? This whole thing was partly her idea."

"That was before you two started getting all cute at dinner."

"That was a show," Wes said. "To get Juliet worked up."

"Seemed to me the only one worked up was you."

Wes was on his feet in a flash. "You know what? I don't need this right now. I have enough shit to deal with."

"Calm down, caveman," Jamal said, lying down where Wes had just been. "Get back here, so I don't kill myself with all this weight."

Waiting a few extra seconds, Wes attempted to bring his blood pressure down a few thousand points.

When he joined Jamal at the weight bench, he looked down at him, catching Jamal's knowing expression.

"What?" Wes asked. "Just spit it out."

"Think about what you're doing. Getting revenge might be what you want in the short term. But what about after you leave Mexico? What will you have then?"

The satisfaction knowing Juliet hurt as badly as he did.

"Football," he said. "That's all I've ever wanted. And I'll finally have it again."

"And that's enough?" Jamal asked with a hint of pity seeping into his words.

"Of course. Why wouldn't it be?"

Jamal opened his mouth as if he wanted to say something, but nothing came out.

"It is," Wes said again with more feeling. "Football is all I need."

Jamal gave Wes a look like he was a lost cause. "Whatever, man. I hope you catch on before it's too late."

Too late for what? Wes was right on time. Everything was falling into place, and he was getting everything he wanted. After waiting so long in agony, he could shove his secret in Juliet's face and finally stop hurting.

That was going to be even sweeter than stepping back on the field this fall.

Chapter Seven

A large tent had been erected on the beach, and beneath was a wooden floor. Chairs rested on the perimeter, where people congregated in a makeshift circle. In the center stood a hotel employee with a microphone and five couples: Juliet and LJ; Avery and her husband, Brandon; Jessica and Ian; Saylor and David; and Hillary and Charles.

The very exuberant hotel employee waved his arms in the air. He wore a white uniform that set off his dark skin and bright smile. "Last call!" he yelled. "Anyone else want to take a shot at proving they love each other more than the rest?"

Heads from the surrounding wedding guests turned to each other in question.

Wes and Teegan were in the mix of people, looking on, waiting for the game to start. She looked up at him with a secret smile.

Jessica called out, and Wes did his best to ignore her. "Tee, Wes." She gestured at where she stood in the center of the circle. "Come on, you guys!"

Both Wes and Teegan shook their heads and mumbled their decline.

They were good right where they were.

"You two are playing, right?" a female voice asked.

He glanced down, watching Juliet's grandmother nudge people out of the way with her wheelchair, stopping at Wes's side.

Etta wore a slick grin. "This is a game for couples. You two are a couple, aren't you?"

"They've got enough people," Wes said.

Etta shouted in a louder voice than her frail body should've been able to project, "We have a late entry! Two more over here!"

All eyes turned their way as Etta pointed her bony fingers at Wes and Teegan. He could've sworn he heard Teegan whimper.

"Excellent." The hotel employee clapped his hands together. "Please, join us."

The crowd opened like a doorway to the participants, leaving Wes and Teegan no choice but to join the group.

Teegan sliced a look at Wes that he was getting used to—like he was a hard-core criminal and she was being locked in isolation with him. He was going to have to do something about that look of hers.

"Yay!" an excited cheer came from the center of the circle.

"Come on, guys!" came another.

Etta gave Wes a hearty shove forward, nearly clipping off his heels with the tires of her wheelchair.

He reached for Teegan's hand, expecting her to bolt, and dragged her to where the other couples stood.

"This is going to be so fun!" Avery said, bouncing on her colorful flip-flops. She reached a hand out to Teegan, which Teegan snatched like a lifeline. Then Avery looked at him with an excited smile. "Hey, Wes."

"Avery," he said unenthusiastically.

"Ladies and gentlemen," the hotel employee said. "My name is Demarco, and I'll be your host this evening. And what kind of host would I be if I didn't make it worth your while?"

A loud cheer came from the crowd, who seemed to know already what they were in for.

"This is, after all, a wedding. It only makes sense for us to have games that test our bride and groom's love for one another.

Am I right?"

More cheers as Juliet smiled and curtsied while LJ pumped his fist in the air.

"First round is a game of Guess That Word Or Phrase. Top three teams will move on to round two and battle it out with a game of Twister. Final round with our top two couples will show us how well they know one another through a series of personal questions."

Oooos and *ahhhhhs* erupted from the crowd.

"My only question now is…" Demarco glanced at his contestants. "Are. You. Ready?"

The wedding guests exploded with shouts of excitement and anticipation.

Avery hugged Teegan, and then turned to Brandon to work on some sort of strategy.

Wes pulled Teegan toward the other side of the floor, away from prying ears.

She looked up at him with eyes that weren't as frightened as they'd been moments ago.

"It's fine," he said. "Just give a bunch of bogus answers, and we'll be out in the first round."

Her eyebrows scrunched. "What? No."

"What do you mean, no?"

"I want to win this," she said.

"You wanna what? Are you crazy?"

She centered her weight on her flat sandals, standing her ground. "I want everyone to think we're compatible. If we get out in the first round, then Hillary and Samara will get what they want. They'll think I'm no good for you. I don't want that. And neither should you. We're dating."

"But we're not really—"

"Don't say it," she said in a singsong voice. "We're in

loooooove, remember? So prove it." Her eyes hardened as she turned back to the center of the room. She glanced over her shoulder at him, and said, "If you want to make Juliet jealous, this is your chance."

She had a point.

A great point that ramped up his need to win immensely.

And that fast, the competitive side of him took hold, making his heart beat a little faster at the prospect.

She went back to where Demarco stood but glanced over her shoulder at Wes with eyes that he could only define as naughty. He stopped dead in his tracks and watched her walk away, frozen by the view in front of him.

Now that's a look he wouldn't mind seeing again. And again. And again. All night.

"All right, folks," Demarco said, kick-starting Wes's brain back into action.

Wes made his way to where chairs had been set up in two rows. Guys on one side and girls on the other, facing each other.

He sat in front of Teegan and waited to be told what to do.

Someone came by and dropped a small contraption in his lap. It was about the size and width of a cell phone. He picked it up and turned it over, noticing the other men being handed a similar item.

Demarco paced in front of the contestants with his hands clasped behind his back. "You may not use any part of the word that appears on the screen, and you may not spell it. Other than that, have fun and let's hope your partner is quick to respond. Ladies will describe the word first. Gentlemen, it is your job to guess what she's describing. It can be anything from pop culture—including TV and movies, landmarks, or even sexual positions. The sky is the limit here, people. The three teams with the most correct answers in the given time will move on to the next round." Demarco smiled. "Everyone ready?"

Sounds of consent passed over the crowd.

Demarco looked at Juliet and LJ. "Our lovely bride and her

fiancé can get us started."

Juliet smoothed her blond ponytail and sat up straighter in her seat. "Okay, let's do this. Just watch me, baby. Guess the first thing that comes to your mind."

LJ pressed something on the device and then lifted it to his forehead, so the screen faced Juliet.

The hotel must've hooked the devices up to some internal network, because as soon as LJ lifted it, a large screen under the tent lit up, counting down.

3...

2...

1...

Go!

The first word on the screen was *Channing Tatum*.

"Uh, okay," Juliet said. "He was in that stripper movie."

"Ron Jeremy," LJ said.

"No. He married Jenna Dewan."

Blank stare from LJ.

"He's super hot."

Still nothing.

"What the hell is the name of that stripper movie?" She paused, then, "Mike. Magic Mike!" She waited, her impatience showing in her rigid posture. "Anything? Anything at all?"

LJ's face was still empty. "I don't know that one."

"Dancing. He and his wife met on Step Up. You saw that, didn't you?"

A shake of LJ's head prompted an eye roll from Juliet.

Wes slid a glance at Teegan, who was holding back a laugh. He winked at her. She covered her giggle behind her hand.

Juliet sliced a look at Wes, and her jaw worked.

"Ugh, forget it." Juliet sent a scowl to LJ. "Next."

LJ pressed the device upward, the screen parallel with the sky, and when he placed it back to his forehead, and new word appeared on the screen.

Jane Austen.

Juliet groaned. "Oh, come on!"

"What? What is it?" LJ said.

"She's an author."

"Oprah," LJ said.

"An *old* author. She wrote Pride and Prejudice, and Sense and Sensibility."

LJ was shaking his head, nothing coming to mind.

Wes started to sweat. If these were the words, they were doomed. He didn't know shit about movies and books. Give him sports stats and sex positions any day.

Wes looked up at the screen, watching the clock tick down from twenty seconds.

Juliet growled. "Next."

The screen read, I'm A Little Teapot.

"This is a children's song," Juliet said. "About a drink that England is known for. Tip me over and pour me out."

"Shit," LJ said. "Something about a kettle, right?"

She was nodding. "Close. Think about it. Something bag. Blank bag."

"Tea." LJ's face twisted in thought. "Teapot. I'm a little teapot!"

"Yes!"

Next on the screen was *Baby Momma.*

Juliet laughed. "If you knock me up and we're not married, I'd be what to you?"

"Begging for child support?" LJ asked.

Snickers sounded from the onlookers.

"No. Come on, think! What would I have in my stomach?"

"A baby."

"And another word for the woman who gave birth to you?"

"Mom. Mammy. Mother. Momma."

Juliet pointed at him when he said the last word. "Yes, put it together."

He said the phrase and they moved on to the next word, which was *Batman*.

Juliet's eyebrows knitted and she let out a strong exhale. "He, uh. I think he's the one that wears all black. He lives somewhere in a city and saves people."

LJ grunted. "That's not vague at all."

"I don't know," Juliet said. "He...he's a superhero. You've watched the movies. I think he lives in a cave."

"Batman?"

"Yes!"

Tom Brady appeared on the screen next.

"Oo, oo," she said, wiggling in her seat. "You know this one. He's an NFL player."

LJ grinned. "Which team?"

"The...the blue and red one. I don't know the name."

"How do you not know?"

Juliet scowled. "I don't, okay?"

Sighing, LJ said, "Did we play them last season?"

Juliet thought about that. "Yeah. I think so. He's married to Gisele."

"Who?"

"Gisele."

"What position?"

"Position?"

The clock counted from five, and with it the crowd started to chant like they were waiting for the New Year's Eve ball to drop in Times Square.

Four.

"On the field!" LJ said.

"Oh. Quarterback," she said.

Three.

"Brady. Tom Brady."

Two.

"Yes!" she shouted.

He snapped the phone forward and back up.

One.

The buzzer went off, ending their turn.

Next group up was Avery and Brandon, who excelled at naming actors, but not so much on the sexual slang, scoring only three points.

Saylor and David, on the other hand, knew their shit when it came to sex and movies. They beat LJ and Juliet with six.

Jessica and her husband were a lost cause, scoring only one point. Same with Hillary and Charles.

Then it was Wes and Teegan's turn.

Christ, his palms were clammy. And the tent felt like it escalated to one hundred degrees.

Teegan didn't appear to be worried. She shot him a bright, confident smile and gave him two thumbs up.

Okay, deep breath. You can do this. She deserves to win. She deserves to show these assholes how amazing she is. Do it for her.

Wait, what? No, you deserve revenge. Do if for you.

Yeah, but Teegan deserves to win more.

Not overanalyzing that thought, he smiled and squared his shoulders before pressing the start button on the device and lifting it to his forehead, screen out.

He heard three dings, then a buzz.

Teegan silently read the word. She looked up at the ceiling in thought, then brought her gaze back to him, and said in a mock Southern accent, "I did not have sexual relations with that woman."

"Bill Clinton."

"Yes. Next."

He flipped the phone down and then back up.

"When it storms, this often happens. Like, rain and bad winds."

"Hurricane."

"No," she said. "It's really loud in the sky."

"Thunder."

"Yes. That plus…"

"Thunder plus…"

"Thor. What does Thor's hammer shoot?"

"Lightning."

Her head was bobbing like he was on the right track. "Put it together."

"Thunder and lightning."

"Yay! Go on."

When the next word came up, she said, "My what brings all the boys to the yard?"

"Your…your…your milkshake!"

Focusing on the phone, no nonsense, as he turned it up and then down, she said, "What sport did you play?"

"Football," he said.

"On what?"

"Grass."

"Another word for grass."

"Turf?"

"Keep going. It's another way of saying a pasture of grass."

Pasture. What was another word for pasture? "Field?"

She rolled her arm over, signaling for him to put the two to-gether.

"Football field?"

"Yes!" she said as he brought the next word up. She started singing, "Everybody was blank fighting."

"Kung Fu."

She nodded vigorously, so he flipped to the next word.

"What the hell!" LJ shouted. "These are too easy! Where's his Jane Aspen and Chauncy whoever!"

"Oh," Teegan said, staring at the screen of the device. Scar-let red overtook her face, and she skated a hesitant glance at the people giggling around them. "Oh, boy."

"What? Just say it. Come on." He knew time was ticking; they needed to get this last one to get ahead of LJ and Juliet in points.

"This is another name for a guy's…you know." She dropped her gaze to his crotch. "That."

A few loud guffaws sounded as he went down the long list of every synonym he could think of, starting with balls, cock, dick, and working his way through the alphabet.

"Keep going." She scooted to the edge of her seat, her body stiff now. It made his pulse kick up another notch. They had to be getting close to the end of their time.

"What else is there?" he asked.

"Uh…" She glanced up, presumably to check on how much time they had left. "What are you?"

"A guy."

She bounced in her seat, impatiently. "Another word for guy."

"Male."

She rolled her arm again for him to keep going, but it was urgent.

"Dude. Man."

She pointed at him.

"Man?"

She nodded. "First word."

"Man…man…"

"What is a steak? The type of food?"

"Meat?" Then it hit him. "Man meat!"

Teegan read the next word and laughed. "Oh, God. Okay. Uh, it's something men really like. Women get down on their knees and…"

No. No way. Seriously?

Without moving his head, he looked out the corner of his eye at the crowd, finding Etta's gaze immediately. The old broad sat in her wheelchair with arms crossed, arrogant smirk on her face.

Was he really going to have to say this with her present?

Etta nodded as if to tell him to go on.

Sure, why not.

"Blow job?" he said.

"Yes!" Teegan said. "Next."

He bent his wrists, then flicked them back up to get to the next word.

"Pamela Anderson was on this show. She wore a red bathing sui—"

"Baywatch."

"Yes!" She was out of her chair and leaping into his arms as the buzzer went off. He enveloped her, holding tight, reveling in the sensation of being a part of a team again. The joy of working together for a common goal. Goddamn, it felt good. And even better with Teegan as his partner.

"We got eight! You were so awesome!" she said, her face glowing up at him.

"So were you." He looked down at her, feeling something blossom. Something sharp and primitive. Something that told him she wasn't just any teammate. He'd never wanted to kiss his teammates before, but he wanted to put his lips on Teegan right now.

Why was this happening?

Keeping his eyes on her mouth, he dipped his head, feeling her surprised breath as he moved in.

They were about an inch apart when someone spoke. "Nice job, guys."

Teegan's eyes snapped open, and she blinked, shifting away from him to scan the people around them.

Juliet stood at their side, watching them intently.

Teegan let go of Wes and slid down his front, landing on her feet. She adjusted the waistband of her skirt and wouldn't meet anyone's gaze.

He spent a few seconds trying to understand the flutter in his chest and why he was so angry that Teegan leaped away from him like he had a disease.

He turned to Juliet. "Seems like there's another couple here just as in love as you and LJ, huh?"

Juliet's satisfied expression faltered a bit, but she recovered. "We'll see."

"We will," he said, getting off on the annoyed look she showed him.

The rest of the game progressed much the same as it went in the first round. Juliet and LJ ended up pulling out five points with words and phrases like schlong, Bugs Bunny, and Vin Diesel. Jessica and Ian didn't have a chance. Neither did Hillary and Charles. The latter spent most of the second round calling each other names and talking down to one another. Avery and Brandon banged out a quick four points in a few seconds, and it looked like they might have been real contenders. But once they got a few pop musicians and eighties movies, they didn't score anymore. It was still enough to put them in second place for now.

It came down to Wes and Teegan.

Once again, she gave him a thumbs-up, and at that moment he wanted to do whatever it would take to win.

She lifted the device to her forehead, and he waited for the game to tick down and show him the first word.

Washing an elephant.

Great. What happened to things like blow job, man meat, and doggie style?

"This is a large, gray, four-legged animal."

Teegan thought for a second before saying, "Elephant?"

"Yes," he said. "Now what do you do when you take a shower?"

"Get clean?"

"Sort of. But what's the act of getting clean? What are you actually doing to get clean?"

"Using soap?"

"Use the soap," he said. "What are you doing with it?"

"Wiping it on myself?"

Jesus, the image of her in the shower rubbing soap all over her body, was one he didn't need to have right now. But goddamn was it a hot-ass vision. Her smooth, slightly tanned skin with rivulets of water coasting over her…

"Was that it?" she said with a confused expression.

He blinked to clear his vision. "Uh, no. Try again."

"Cleaning. Bathing. Showering," she rattled off words.

"When you want your car to get clean, what do you do to it?"

"Wash it." Then her eyes sparked. "Washing an elephant?"

"Yes. Next."

Riding a carousel.

Really?

"This is a thing that goes around in a circle and has horses on it that goes up and down."

"Carousel."

"When you're on it, what are you doing?"

"Riding it."

"Yeah, say it all."

"Riding a carousel."

"Next."

The two that came up after were fairly easy—*hard hat* and *Harry Potter*. They banged those out pretty quick. Then *missionary* came up.

"When we're having sex," he said, "and you're on the bottom, and I'm on top. What's that called?"

Her face flushed and she said through a strangled voice, "Magic?"

Wes stilled. Magic? Did she really just say that?

Then another vision came over him. Empty wine bottles. Wrinkled sheets. The huge bed in their suite. Just Wes and Teegan, not giving a damn about anything in the outside world besides each other.

Yeah, he could make it magic for her.

She should know what that feels like. A man wanting her. Desiring her. Making her feel like she's everything. He couldn't believe no one had shown her that already.

The crowd was completely silent, making her realize what she said, and she quickly threw out, "Shit. I mean, sex. Uh, lovemaking. Doing it. We'd be doing it."

"Yes, we would," he said with a smile. "What's the position?"

She swallowed. "Mi-missionary."

"Good girl," he said. "Next."

Hummer appeared on the screen, but the buzzer went off before he could finish.

Demarco approached, reaching for Wes's hand and then Teegan's. He extended them into the air like prize-winning boxers after a long fight in the ring. "Congratulations, folks! Well played. Three couples are moving onto the next round. Twister, here we come!"

The crowd cheered.

Teegan's terrified expression was back. *Twister*? she mouthed.

He pulled his hand out of Demarco's to reach for her. "Piece of cake. We've got this."

Glancing down at their connection, a slow smile broke across her lips. "Yes. We do."

Chapter Eight

Teegan was face up with each foot on a green tile at the end of the Twister board, one hand on a yellow in the next row up, and another stretched a row further onto blue. She felt exactly like she probably looked—a demented crab trying to crawl to salvation. Wes was slightly better. He was next to her, looking down at their mat as if he was doing a complicated yoga move with shoulders and legs braced wide.

Pretty hot, actually. Holding himself over something underneath him. Something like…a woman perhaps? And what do you know? Teegan was a woman. She would totally stand in for that role if needed.

Juliet and LJ were on their mat to the right. Juliet was facedown in a position similar to Wes, and LJ was on the opposite end of the mat in a crouched-type position. Each of them had wobbled a bit on the last move, but they held on.

Teegan couldn't wait to see both of them on their asses in defeat.

Avery and Brandon were on the farthest mat, looking like a twisted pretzel about to tear in half. Her face was red, and she was breathing heavy, while he had an expression of deep concentration.

Teegan peered back at Wes, reveling in that warmth she'd grown accustomed to feeling when she was near him.

This was a good game for him. His athleticism definitely showed. As did his muscles while he held each position. His biceps contracted, pulling his shirtsleeve tight as if it might rip. The veins in his thick neck strained and his calves flexed into well-formed, solid bulges. But she wasn't going to think about that right now because if she did, she'd get hot and bothered, and then she'd lose her ability to remain in her current position.

They had to win.

"Yellow hand," Demarco called out.

She passed a glance to her left and slowly slid her palm from the blue circle down one row, breathing a sigh of relief. Okay, a small sigh. Her abs burned like someone was branding them with a George Foreman grill.

An arm crossed over her chest and then Wes's face came into view above her. He landed his hand on the yellow to her far left. "Couldn't reach over there," he said. His face was inches from hers, their chests nearly brushing. "Sorry."

Talk about missionary position. Boy, oh boy.

"N-no," she said. "It's fine. I'm good. I mean, you're good. We're good. Everything's good."

Perfectly, exquisitely, awesomely good.

A soft laugh from Wes, then, "I agree, we are good." His gaze skimmed down her body—or at least what he could see in their situation—and his expression seemed to take on a new shape. A deeper, sharper, seductive one.

Which couldn't be right, could it? She had to be misreading his face. Maybe he was just concentrating hard on not squashing her. Nearly 300 pounds would be a lot for her to take if he fell on her.

It would be a lot to take another way too. Though she wouldn't complain one bit.

The thought of Wes on top of her, all the way, skin to skin, sent a shockwave of need through her. Of course, she'd fantasized about it, and being this close, their bodies almost touching, with that sexy look in his eyes…it was a lot to take in.

Take in. Would you cool it with taking him in?

She let out a shaky exhale as her stomach fluttered, which made her almost crumble onto her backside. She quickly righted herself, slicing her pelvis upward, causing it to bump into his.

Oh, God.

He jolted from the impact and made an *oomph* sound. His eyes slammed closed for a second, but he didn't back away, and he didn't lift his lower stomach off hers.

She was ashamed to admit how much she liked his parts against hers.

All she had to do was rub a little—

His eyes widened through a ragged groan.

Good Lord, Teegan. Get your head on straight!

This was Wes she was talking about. He didn't want her that way. He was here because of his ex. Nothing more. No matter how badly she wanted it to be more.

"You okay?" he asked, his hot breath against her cheek that was utter torture.

"Fine," she said.

"There's that word again. The one you use when you're anything but fine."

She laughed lightly. "It's nothing," she said. "Honestly."

You'd think I was a complete nut if you knew the thoughts running rampant through my mind right now, you sexy yoga beast.

His eyebrows lowered. "You have the weirdest expression right now. You sure you're okay?"

Great. She misread his expression, thinking he had the hots for her; and when she actually *did* have the hots for him, he thought she was confused or constipated.

"I'm good. Thanks."

"Oh, this one should be interesting," Demarco said, reading

from the game spinner. "How about red hand?"

Red? Did he just say red? That was on the opposite end of the board!

"Damn," Wes said. "Guess that means I have to get off of you."

No, you don't.

He does if you want to win.

Win? Who cares about winning?

"I guess so," she said. "I mean if you want to. Or don't want to. It's totally your choice."

God almighty, shut up!

Wes leaned in and kissed her. Kissed her! A quick, tiny brush of his lips against hers, but she still nearly threw herself at him. The game be damned.

But then he was gone, leaving her to feel the lasting tingle. She licked her lips, wanting to savor any tiny sliver of him on her tongue. Wes glided a straight leg to the other side of the board, which also moved his crotch from hers.

Bye-bye, Wes's crotch. It was so pleasant meeting you! Let's do this again soon!

Before she could mourn too long, she heard Juliet call from her right. "You're not giving up, are you, Teegan?"

You wish. In a swift move, Teegan flipped over so that she faced the board, similar to the pose Wes did earlier, and she stretched as far as she could across the mat without letting her stomach touch the ground. She got a few fingers onto the red circle. Stretching a little further, she managed most of her hand.

"Nice!" Wes said.

The elation she felt from his vote of confidence shouldn't have made her as happy as it did. But hell, she'd take it. And bask in it.

Juliet's lips formed into what looked like disdain. She mimicked Teegan's move, but she seemed to do it while flaunting her ass in the air.

LJ sent an approving glance his fiancée's way. "You know I love it when you do that, baby."

But Juliet wasn't looking at LJ. Her lusty, bedroom eyes were locked on Wes.

Oh, hell no.

Irrational jealousy took hold of Teegan, making her want to strangle her sorority sister. So that's how it was going to be?

All right, then. Teegan wasn't as natural at exuding sex the way Juliet was, but she'd try.

Demarco called the next color, which caused Teegan to slide her right leg up two rows. Her butt hoisted into the air in a position similar to doggie style. She popped up onto her tiptoes to over-exaggerate the move, and she sent a self-satisfied smirk at Juliet. The other woman's jaw dropped. She reciprocated by flicking her hair over her shoulder with a twist of her head, then arching her back. The shit-eating grin she shot Teegan almost made Teegan forget about this game. She wanted to turn it into another type of competition—full-on MMA in a cage.

"What are you doing?" Wes asked at a volume only Teegan could hear.

"What?" she asked.

"You. What are you doing?"

"Nothing," she said. "Trying to win."

"You sure about that?"

The next color Demarco called made Juliet smirk. She lowered herself into a crouched position, then twisted so that she faced the ceiling, and then rolled her hips in a wave motion up and down. And again. And again.

Ugh. No fair. That looked exactly like she was humping the air. How was Teegan supposed to compete with that?

Teegan moved her hand a row down, still facing the mat, and she tried gyrating her pelvis a few times.

"Seriously, what the hell are you doing?" Wes asked, transitioning into his next pose. "You look like you're having some sort of episode."

Yeah, a sexy-stripper episode.

"Do you wanna win this thing or not?" he asked.

"Of course I do. What about you? Do you want to win?"

"Yeah."

"Really?"

"Yes, really," he said through gritted teeth. "Why are you saying it like that?"

She attempted a shrug, but it was more of a shift of her shoulders given her current strained position. "Seems to me like you're more concerned with that bobbing ripe peach over there."

Wes blinked a few times, then his mouth quirked. "Peach?"

"You are, aren't you?"

Demarco said something she missed.

Wes moved into a squat as he said, "Move your left leg up to red." This caused her to do a plank with legs spread wide, almost into a split. She let out a strangled groan. Real comfortable on the joints. Not to mention she wasn't flexible.

She glanced up at Juliet, who was in some contorted pose with her foot up by her ear as graceful and boneless as a squid.

Damn. Talk about flexible.

"You look good in that position," Wes said.

She swung a look his way. That glint was back in his eyes. The one that melted her insides and flipped her stomach over.

If he only knew what that look did to her. And if only she could do something about it.

Then the crowd shouted a mix of elation and disappointment, which reluctantly tugged Teegan's gaze from her hot partner.

Brandon had fallen onto the mat, landing on his stomach, before he slammed a fist down. Avery frowned as she crawled to her husband and kissed him on the top of the head.

"Too bad!" Demarco said. He turned to Teegan and Wes, and also to LJ and Juliet. "Well, that's it, folks. Here are your last two couples!"

Everyone around them hooted and whistled in delight.

They did it! They survived Twister. And they were one step closer to showing all these hoo-hahs how into each other they were.

"Let's move onto the final round!"

• • •

"There are three questions for the ladies to answer, and then three questions for the gentlemen," Demarco explained. "No cheating, please. No hand signals or telepathic clues. You either know your partner, or you don't."

Four chairs were placed in the center of the tent, grouped in twos. Juliet and Teegan were seated together, and LJ and Wes across from them.

Each female had a black marker and a white poster in her lap. As Wes took his seat, Teegan winked at him. He smiled back, trying to ignore the sick feeling stirring in his stomach because they knew absolutely nothing about each other.

His pulse immediately took off into a sprint. Shit. How were they going to do this? The first two rounds were one thing, just staying close and acting in love. He even kissed her once for good measure. But answering personal questions?

They were fucked. Juliet, LJ, and everyone else in this tent would know it was a setup. That he'd convinced Teegan to bring him to the wedding. That he wasn't in love with her.

He wasn't, of course. But that didn't mean all these people needed to know that.

She must have seen something in his face because she leaned forward to pat his knee. "You've got this," she said.

Her confidence in him was horribly misplaced. If they didn't pull this off, they'd both be screwed. And not in the enjoyable sense.

He glanced across at Juliet, who was watching him with an odd expression. Like she could read his thoughts. Her eyes narrowed slightly, and her eyes were too perceptive. It was her *I know what you're up to* look. He'd never been able to hide anything from her. She'd always known everything, even before he knew it.

Not this time.

They didn't call him the Ice Box for nothing.

He brought his attention back to Teegan and smiled wide. Even if he got every question wrong, he'd go down fighting. He'd have Juliet panting in her seat by the time he was done—it was crucial.

"Ladies," Demarco began. "First question. When it comes to romance, which of these would your man say you prefer: being totally out of control, being completely in control, or to be controlled? You, ladies. Which would your man say that you prefer?"

Juliet threw a look at LJ with hooded eyes and a saucy smile. He giggled—yes, giggled—in his chair. Christ, what a clown he was.

Teegan looked up to the ceiling of the tent in thought, then she came back to Wes. She stared at him like she was trying to decide on her response. Or maybe trying to picture them together.

He stared right back. Control. You like control.

Anyone who knew her would say it. He didn't know much about her personally, but he did know that.

She must have made her decision because she started writing her response with the black marker.

"Okay," Demarco said. "It appears the ladies are done. Now we're going to turn to the men. LJ, we'll start with you. Would you say your beautiful bride likes being totally out of control, being completely in control, or being controlled?"

LJ still wore a big, goofy grin. "Totally out of control. She's an animal in the sack, D."

Teegan made a choking noise, then coughed to cover it up.

Demarco's eyes bulged as he passed a look over the crowd. Onlookers snickered and looked away, hiding their smirks.

Wes shook his head. Such a tool. Juliet's parents were here for crying out loud. Not to mention, Juliet was a control freak to the tenth degree. She'd want to be completely in control. When she and Wes had been together, he couldn't stand that. She always had to handle him. Tell him when and where to go. Where to touch her. How to touch her. Which was fine to an extent. He'd wanted to satisfy her. But sometimes it would've been nice for Wes to be able to let loose. Be spontaneous.

Juliet's bright expression dimmed as she sighed and turned her sign around. "Completely in control," she said. "Why would you even say out of control? You know I like to call the shots."

LJ's grin dropped. "But, babe…"

Juliet put a palm in the air. "Stop."

"Wes," Demarco said. "What say you? How does Teegan prefer it?"

He hesitated, giving himself a few extra seconds. "I'm going with being completely in control."

Teegan stuck out her bottom lip and lifted her sign. "Be controlled."

Hey now. That quick, he didn't care they'd gotten that one wrong. Hell, he reveled in that little nugget of information. His mind flashed to a scene where Teegan was beneath him, a look of complete abandon on her face, her body his for the taking. He pictured her arms over her head and her back arched, which brought her full breasts closer to his mouth. He was welcome to do whatever he wanted to pleasure her.

His eyes gazed down her body to the items he was just imagining. They were bound behind a neckline that went straight across her chest. No cleavage to speak of, but the silhouette showed they were full and heavy. His hands itched to reach out and cup them. He loved when a woman's breasts filled his large palms.

Someone cleared their throat.

Wes brought his attention up to Teegan's face. Her eyebrows were raised, and cheeks were darkening.

Shit. He flung a glance at the faces around them. Most were smiling in a way that told him they'd seen his little fantasy. Juliet wore a sneer and tossed her ponytail over one shoulder as she whipped her head away.

"Getting steamy in here now, folks!" Demarco said. "Let's move on to the next question and see what else these lovers reveal." He looked at the women and asked, "What was the first thing your guy said to you after sex that had nothing to do with sex?"

Teegan tapped the end of the marker against her chin and then wrote her response. Juliet was a lot quicker, not needing the time to think.

Demarco paced behind their chairs, glancing at Juliet and Teegan's answers. When they were done writing, he said, "LJ, go ahead."

LJ looked confused for a moment, so Demarco repeated the question. "What was the first thing you said to Juliet after sex that had nothing to do with sex?"

The other man shrugged. "I don't know. Wake up?"

Jesus Christ. Really?

The crowd broke out into loud, obnoxious laughter. Demarco, too, seemed to be struggling for air.

Juliet rolled her eyes and shook her head. "What is *wrong* with you?"

"What?" LJ asked. "I don't know what I said."

"How about"—she turned her sign around—"I love you?"

"Oh." LJ pointed at her sign. "Yeah, I guess that."

Crossing her arms, Juliet positioned her body slightly away from her fiancé.

"Wes, what do you think?" Demarco asked. "What did you say to Teegan after sex that didn't have anything to do with sex?"

"I love you," he said without giving it much thought.

Teegan's lips spread wide, showing her card. "I love you."

A collective sigh of the female persuasion sounded to his right. When he glanced that way, Jessica, Saylor, and Avery were blinking faster than normal with their hands gathered together under their dainty chins. At least he and Teegan were doing a good job deceiving her friends.

Wes turned to his date, catching a look that was enough to crack his chest open. She was shining. Radiating with happiness. The attention from the crowd. The satisfaction of making them think they were in love. It filled him with happiness to give her what she wanted.

"Gentlemen, last one," Demarco said. "Please turn and look at me." Once they did, he said, "Now, tell me, what color eyes your girl has."

Wes concentrated on his image of Teegan. Her smiling face. The delight she carried around with her on a seemingly permanent basis. And her…blue eyes. Yes, they were blue. A deep, rich color like the ocean just beyond this tent. How had he not noticed how unique the color was until this moment?

He said his response, earning him another grin from Teegan. He'd expected it, and yet it still nearly knocked the breath out of him. Damn, he enjoyed seeing her smile because of something he said or did.

"LJ," Demarco prompted.

"Uh," he said, leg bobbing in place. "B-brown. I'm going with brown."

Juliet flew out of her seat, throwing the poster and marker onto the ground. She trudged over them with her wedge sandals and kept going.

"Babe?" LJ said. "They're brown, aren't they?"

She spun back at him with a look that would've scared Godzilla. "Blue!" she shouted. "They're blue! Just like yours! See!" Juliet used her fingers to open her eyes wider.

"Hmm," LJ said. "You're right. They are."

Juliet cocked her head like she couldn't believe her fiancé could be so dense, then thrust her hands into the air and started to stomp away again.

"We're winning!" Teegan said quietly, getting out of her chair. He got up, too, and went to her.

They hugged as they'd done earlier, and he realized how incredible it felt with her in his arms. How much he'd missed her there until this moment. How he'd like to stay that way for the rest of the game. And then after.

What was happening to him?

She pulled back and gazed up at him. "You're doing so great," she said so only he could hear. "Thank you."

"I've got a great partner." And that was it. She was great. More than great. And everyone here needed to know it.

Sliding an arm around her back for support and burying a hand into her hair, he lowered his head. Didn't think about what they were doing, simply let his instincts guide him. He placed his lips on hers, softly at first. Testing it out. She stiffened in his arms, but only for a second before she softly moaned and relaxed. Her arms came around to clasp the back of his neck, and he almost howled at the delicious feel of her body against his. He dove back in, applying varying pressure, learning every spot that ignited her desire.

Teegan tilted her head and opened her mouth slightly. He shouldn't take what she was offering in front of all these people, but at the moment he didn't care. Wes slid his tongue out for one slow swipe against hers. She whimpered and gripped his neck hard enough to bruise. In any other circumstance, he would've grabbed her ass, lifted her up, and had her against the nearest wall. But since they were here with a single mission—and it had nothing to do with either of them getting off—he slowed his pace, placing gentle kisses along her cheek and jawline before drawing back and looking at her.

Her eyes were unfocused and her lips a little swollen. He

wanted to carry her back to their suite right now so that none of the other men could witness how delectable she looked.

"That…that was…" She touched her lips. "Wow."

"We've done that a million times, remember?" he whispered.

She sucked in a quick breath and her body tensed as she remembered where they were. Her gaze skated to the right, toward the gathered group watching them intently.

Wes cupped her cheek, trying to soothe her. "Teegan."

She brought her eyes back to his, that familiar frightened look coming with it.

"That was better than wow," he said. "And all these people know it."

Teegan looked past him. "Juliet knows it now too."

He looked over his shoulder at a very pissed-off Juliet. She marched toward them, brushing past him with a huff, and sank into her seat with folded arms.

Excellent. This evening was getting better and better.

Placing a kiss on the tip of Teegan's nose, he said, "Let's finish this. You and me. Are you in?"

She smiled slow and wide. "Yeah, I'm in."

They settled into their chairs, Juliet more reluctant than the rest, and Demarco instructed the ladies to hand the poster board to the men.

Staring at the blank paper, Wes waited for Demarco to begin.

"Would you say your woman would agree or disagree with the phrase size matters?"

Wes chuckled, loud and confident. If there was one thing he was, it was large. He quickly wrote *AGREE* and then stood. Lifting his arms in the air, he flexed his biceps and spun in a circle, letting his height and width speak for him.

Sounds of approval exploded all around them.

Juliet rolled her eyes while LJ grinned.

Through a laugh, Teegan said, "Size definitely matters."

"Goddamn right it does," Wes said, flipping his card around.

Juliet and LJ got that one right too.

"Gentlemen, what's the very first thing you do before going to bed?" Demarco asked.

Wes and LJ wrote their answers, and when they were done, Demarco asked Juliet to give her answer.

She looked right at Wes, and said, "We make mad, passionate love, then we go to sleep."

Wes waited for the knife in his gut her words should've caused. But for the first time in he couldn't remember how long—there was nothing. She could've said they play a round of Madden on Xbox for as unenthused as he was with her response. Though, honestly, video games probably would've excited him a little.

"Perhaps I should rephrase the question," Demarco said to Juliet. "What is the first thing LJ does *before* he goes to bed."

"We make—"

"*Before*," Demarco said. "Before he gets in bed."

Blank stare, then, "He looks at me?"

Demarco directed a tired expression at LJ. "What did you write down?"

LJ flipped his card around. "I take a piss."

Laughter from the crowd had become the normal response at this point. So was Juliet's eye roll.

"Final response, guys," Demarco said to Teegan and Wes. "Teegan, what is the first thing Wes does before he goes to bed?"

Juliet leaned over to Teegan as if she was going to impart some secret, but she said it loud enough for everyone to hear. "Wes and I hardly ever made it to the bed—usually it was the kitchen counter, floor, or couch—so I can't help you with this one." She wore a self-satisfied grin as Teegan's mouth opened in disbelief. Then her eyes filled with uncertainty and her face went white.

"Juliet," Wes said in warning. She could say that stuff to him all day, but Teegan was off-limits.

"What?" she said going for innocent but failed miserably. "It's the truth. You know it as much as I do."

Teegan wilted in her chair.

He wanted to string Juliet up by her long blond ponytail. She knew exactly what she was doing and how it would affect Teegan. And it made him angry. Beyond angry. The need to protect Teegan from any kind of harassment took over. Which was ironic since he was the one who'd put her in this position in the first place. He guessed that was why he felt protective now—all of this was his doing.

"Hey," he said, trying to get Teegan's attention.

She flung a halfhearted look his way.

"We've got this," he said with a smile.

One corner of her mouth tipped up, then dropped. "Yeah."

"Teegan," he said. "Come on. I need you."

She perked up a little at that.

"More than you realize." Probably more than he realized too.

She sat up a little taller.

Juliet passed a look between then, made a sound of disgust, then turned back to her fiancé.

"Okay," Teegan said. "I say that you brush your teeth before you go to bed."

"Good girl." He twisted his response around. His sign said, *I brush my teeth.*

Jessica and Avery dashed to where they stood, pulling Teegan out of her chair. The three of them jumped up and down, holding hands like kids playing Ring Around the Rosie. Then Saylor screeched and joined the circle, the group talking over one another with their congratulations.

That was it. They'd won the game. They'd proved to everyone

that they were the most in love couple at the wedding. Beating out all the other real couples, even the bride and groom. He was getting exactly what he wanted. He was showing Juliet he'd moved on. He was happy with someone else.

Then why did he feel hollow? Why did he have an ache in his chest that told him he was missing something?

Like having someone as special as Teegan in his life for real.

Chapter Nine

Man, what a rush. Teegan was so light she could be floating. If no one believed she and Wes were in love before, they did now.

Demarco had signaled the DJ, and a thumping beat instantly kicked up. Everyone descended into the center of the floor, dancing and grooving to the tempo. The house lights dimmed as strobe lights flashed and smoke drifted around their feet. Wedding guests closed in, circling Teegan and Wes, increasing the temperature to the scorching likes of a packed downtown club.

People fought to get around one another to share their congratulations with her and Wes. She felt like a rock star. If this was what being in love was all about, sign her up!

Teegan snuck a look at her partner, who had now drifted about five people away. He looked content accepting everyone's praise. Composed like always. This must be what he felt like after every game—adoring fans vying for a mere millisecond of his time. She saw the appeal.

He must have felt her gaze because his eyes found hers and held. There was something sweet about the way he looked at her. Adoring and proud, even. It gave her courage, which she'd lacked the last day or two.

Teegan pressed the person in front of her aside, making her way toward him. She shimmied around an older couple dancing close together, never taking her gaze off Wes. He mirrored her move, excusing himself from one of his teammates to make his way toward her.

Eyes locked, they met in the center of the crowded group, bodies bumping into them, knocking Teegan slightly off balance. She placed a hand on his solid chest as she lifted onto her toes and roughly pulled his face down to hers. She kissed him. Full out, before she lost the nerve, and without worrying about what he'd think or if anyone else was watching.

She was so high, she was going to live for the moment.

His large hand threaded into her hair, holding her face against his. His other arm went around her waist, and he lifted her off the ground so he could straighten to his full height.

Kissing Wes was like nothing she'd ever felt. It was soft. It was hard. It was rough. And it was slow. Everything and anything she could imagine. The light stubble around his mouth created delicious friction as he devoured her with punishing pressure. His arm tightened around her, locking her against him.

Her heart pounded in her chest so hard she was sure he felt it. Or maybe that was his heart, who knew? All that mattered at that moment was their connection.

Wes drew back, placing his forehead against hers, inhaling breaths as if he'd just completed the forty-yard dash. "What are you doing to me?"

"I don't know," she said. "But I like it."

The chuckle he let out reverberated against her breasts, causing a thrill to race up her spine. Her body thrummed with energy, her nerve endings on full alert.

"I like it too," he said, his breath fanning her lips. "A lot."

He kissed her again, this time opening and sliding his tongue in on contact. She welcomed the warm sensation, already meeting him halfway. Damn, he was perfect. In everything. His heated skin, his masculine scent, just the sheer taste of him was driving her to madness.

How many times had he danced with her in the past? So many.

And how many times had she imagined making out like this with him? Every single one.

If the pearly gates opened up and swallowed her in the next few seconds, she'd willingly fall into the unknown as a happy, thoroughly kissed woman.

The hand that had been in her hair was now quickly working its way down her side, where Wes gripped her thigh, his fingers digging into her bare skin, and he roughly hoisted it up to rest against his hip. This, of course, opened her apex to the vital part of him that was a hell of a lot harder than she'd remembered it being moments ago.

Ahhhhh, yeah! Give me some of that extra-long goodness right now!

"You wanna get out of here?" he asked.

"Hell yes, I do," she said, feeling bolder than she'd ever been in her life. It was Wes. He was making her feel like a wanton, sexy woman.

He released the hold on her leg, letting it dangle along with her other, then slowly lowered her to the ground. Wes glided his hand down her arm to wrap his fingers around hers, and he started to lead her out of the center of the group toward the back entrance of the resort.

All she kept thinking about was sex. Low-down, dirty, freaky sex.

Please, please, please let me experience a night of wild, crazy, break-the-furniture sex with him. Just once, that's all I ask.

They had escaped the dance floor, the low din of the music a distant memory now and were en route to the scarcely lit back patio of the hotel when someone stepped in front of them.

"Hey, guys," Misty said, with an unreadable expression. "Where ya headed?" Her gaze dropped to their joined hands.

Wes snatched his hand away so quick that Teegan almost fell forward from the force. He crossed his arms. "Just going for a walk, why?"

"That was quite a show you two put on earlier," she said. "Almost had me convinced you were in love."

"You know what we're doing," he said, scanning the area around them. No one was near, but he still lowered his voice. "You know it's not real. It's just a show."

Pain cut through Teegan's midsection. It was stupid, she knew. They'd set this whole sham up together. But it still hurt to hear him say it out loud. So matter-of-factly.

Hadn't he felt *anything* when they kissed?

Misty glanced at Teegan, seeming to come to some conclusion if the flat line of her lips was any indication. She pointed at her brother. "You promised me no one would get hurt."

He shot his hands up. "No one is."

"You sure about that?" Misty asked, sliding another look at Teegan.

"Yeah, I am," he said. "But we won't be if you keep going on about it, you damn nag."

Oh, shit. He was about to kick the hornet's nest.

Misty's eyes hardened as she sized her brother up. "I'm giving up valuable time with my husband to help you out here, you horse's ass. I demand a little respect."

Wes scanned the quiet area, seeming to notice Misty was alone. "Why? Where's Jim?"

"He's in his Rick Grimes costume waiting for me in bed. We paid extra for the gun holster with a revolver that shoots vodka. I don't have a lot of time, so listen up."

"There's nothing to hear," he said. "I told you, we're good."

Misty pointed a finger at Teegan. "She's definitely not good."

"Me?" Teegan said. "What about me?"

"Are you blind?" Misty asked Wes.

"About what?" he said.

"What about me?" Teegan tried again.

Misty grunted. "She's in love with you, you big turd blossom. Can't you see that?"

"What?" he said, swinging confused eyebrows Teegan's way.

"No, I'm not!" Teegan nearly shouted.

"She is," Misty insisted to Wes. "She's loved you since college. After you took her to the Christmas formal our sophomore year."

"I don't!" Teegan said, her throat constricting. "I swear I don't! Didn't. Won't. Whatever!"

This was going to ruin everything. Teegan just wanted sex. That was all. Well, it wasn't *all*. But if sex was what Wes was willing to give, then she'd take it. But if he thought she loved him, that she'd get attached, he'd never touch her again.

"Come on," Misty said. "You can't see how bad she wants your sex and candy?"

"My what?" he asked.

"I do not!" Teegan cried.

"She wants it from you bad. For the long term."

Wes massaged his forehead. "She can't," he said to Misty. "She doesn't."

His sister shrugged. "She does."

Stomping her foot, Teegan said, "Can we please stop talking about me like I'm not here?"

Her outburst didn't help. Brother and sister continued on, so Teegan found a chair at a nearby table and dropped into it.

Was she in love with Wes? She'd always been attracted to him. She'd always cared about him.

But love?

"What's going to happen when you two leave this wedding?" Misty asked her brother. "Have you thought about that?"

"We'll go back to our lives. Like things were before."

Misty lowered her chin and looked at Wes like he'd just said he wanted to try out for the cheerleading squad. Then she turned pointed eyes on Teegan. "You good with that?"

"Oh, now it's my turn to talk?"

Misty nodded, all serious.

"It'll be fine," she said. "He'll be in Houston; I'll go back to New York. It'll be like nothing ever happened."

Again, that pain wouldn't subside. But this was how it had to be. What did she expect? To be swept away this weekend into a fairy tale?

Those kinds of things didn't happen to her. Especially not with a guy like Wes.

Misty laughed, but it wasn't a happy sound. It was more like a sharp bark from a rabid pit bull. "I knew this was gonna happen. You know, I hate being the voice of reason around here. Neither one of you thought this thing through." She was shaking her head and exhaling hard through her nose. "What's gonna happen when you two aren't together after this weekend?"

Teegan shrugged. "We'll go back to—"

"No, you're not hearing me," she said, eyes hardening. "What about *after* all the stories you've been telling people about how in love you two are? What happens next week when all of a sudden you're not in love? Huh? Have you thought about that?"

Shit. No, she hadn't. She was only focused on the moment. This weekend. The bliss of the here and now.

Catching her expression, Misty looked up to the dark, cloudless sky. "Right." She brought her attention back to Teegan and let out a long, drawn-out sigh. "I don't want to lose you over this."

"You won't."

Her lips lifted into the semblance of a smile, but it missed its mark. "I've heard that before."

"I'm not Juliet," she said. "And this isn't real. We're just... playing a part this weekend. Sure, maybe we got a little carried away tonight, but as Wes said, we're good. There's no reason to worry."

Misty was silent a few moments, chewing on Teegan's words. "You promise?"

Teegan laid a hand on her heart. "I swear."

Misty finally let her worried best friend façade fall away, and she held her arms out. "Come here."

Teegan made her way to Misty so they could exchange a tight hug.

After they released, Misty turned to Wes. "Keep it in your shorts, Willy Wonka. Nobody needs a ride down Chocolate Mountain this weekend, you hear me?"

• • •

Wes watched as Teegan paced their hotel room, picking up things and putting them down somewhere else. She wasn't straightening up since one, the room wasn't a mess, and two, most of the items she placed didn't end up where they belonged. Like her bathing suit. She retrieved it from the balcony outside, brought it in and draped it over the massive modern black headboard. He didn't own a bikini, but he imagined that wasn't where women normally hung them.

"You okay?" he asked from his seat on the sofa, legs kicked out in front of him, one ankle over the other.

"Huh?" she said, digging her heels into the wood floor as if she just now realized he was still in the room. "Oh, yeah. I'm fine." Then she winced, probably remembering what he'd said about that word before.

He spun around on the sofa and placed his feet on the floor before patting the spot next to him. "Come. Sit."

She hesitated, glancing at the lone flip-flop in her hand, then placed it on the end of the mattress and made her way toward him. She dropped down with a huff. He noticed how far away she sat. Nearly on the opposite side of the sofa. Instead of asking her to move, he did the work for her. Scooting across to her side of the couch, he slipped an arm behind her and pulled her into him.

She took in a breath and held it.

"Talk to me."

Not meeting his eyes, she exhaled. "I...I want you to forget about everything Misty said. It was embarrassing and wholly untrue. I don't...love you. Or want your sex candy or anything like that. So, don't worry, this doesn't have to get weird or anything. We don't even have to have sex. No pressure. I promise."

"Hmm," he said from deep in his throat. "That's too bad."

She stiffened and zipped surprised eyes his way.

Wes took a finger and traced lazy circles above her knee. "I want you to know how much I enjoyed kissing you."

Teegan's eyes expanded. "You did?"

He nodded, letting the circles climb higher up her smooth thigh, stopping just below where her skirt ended. "In fact, I'd like to do it again."

"You would?"

Nodding again, he said, "Would you like that? Me kissing you?" His finger continued its ascent, now treading up to the juncture where her leg connected with her body, trailing the fabric up with it.

"Y-yes," she said breathily. "I would."

"Just on the lips? Or...other places too?" He led his finger inward, letting the trajectory of his path toward her apex insinuate his meaning.

Her stomach sucked in. "Oh, good Lord."

"You were so demanding earlier when we were outside. What happened? Why so shy now?"

"'Cause that...that was the heat of the moment. This...this..."

"Isn't?" he asked. "It's not hot enough for you?" In one swift move, he twisted and fell onto his back, pulling her on top of him, cowgirl style. The fire he saw in her gaze as she peered down at him was enough to confirm that she wanted him just as much as he wanted her. "How's this? Hot enough yet?"

She swallowed hard. "Good. Good. Real good."

He let his eyes roam over their position, feeling desire stir low in his stomach. "I think we can spice it up more, don't you?" One press of his hips upward and her breath hitched. "What do you think, Teegan?"

She was nodding, hesitant at first. Then she snapped out of the fog she was in, and she sat up straighter, which rubbed exactly where he needed.

He groaned, and she smiled like she was satisfied with herself. And she did it again.

"Does this mean we can have wild, crazy sex now?"

He laughed loud and uncontrolled. Man, it felt good to let loose. "Do you want to have wild, crazy sex with me?"

"More than anything," she said, her eyes sharp and alert.

That was more than enough of an invitation for him.

Then she pouted slightly. "Aren't you a little worried about Misty? I don't want to hurt her. This"—she gestured to their connected bodies—"would definitely hurt her."

"We won't," he said. "We both know what we're doing. We're adults. And besides..." He ground his hips again, causing her eyes to close and head to loll back. "She's not here right not. And I want you."

She looked at him with a slightly hooded gaze. "I want you too."

It was a risky move, he knew it. But he was getting to the point that he didn't care. Somehow Teegan had come out of nowhere and ramped him up more than he'd ever thought possible. She was so responsive, reacting in a way that no other woman had. After years of women throwing themselves at him because of his status, even while he was in a relationship, here Teegan was making him feel important because of who he was, not what he did or what he could buy her.

Wes bent forward, placing his hand at the base of her neck. He lined his lips up with hers, but she threw a finger up to stop him.

Drawing back, she said, "If we're going to do this, I have one condition."

"Name it." Anything so he could get on with what he was about to do.

"We don't tell Misty," she said.

"No problem." He leaned in.

"Ever," she continued, making him pause. "Like, even if she tortures us. Don't give in."

Laughing, he said, "I doubt it'll come to that."

She touched her chin to her chest. "Uh, hello? Have you met your sister? She's relentless."

"Good point. Okay, my lips are sealed."

There was a saucy curl to her smile as one eyebrow quirked. "Well, I hope they'll open a little bit. At least for the next hour or so."

"You don't have to worry about that." He dove in, locking his lips with hers. They were soft and sweet. Purely Teegan. His hands roamed her body as she moved slightly above him, stroking him through their clothes.

"Are we really going to do this?" she asked, her breaths growing heavy.

"Yeah, why? You having second thoughts already? Christ, woman. We just got started."

"Nah," she said, putting her arms around him. "Just hard to believe, that's all."

"Why?" his word was mumbled mid-kiss.

Her shoulders went up once. "It's you."

Wes pulled back to look at her face. "What does that mean?"

Another shrug. "Isn't it obvious?"

"No."

Her eyes glimmered. "You're Wes Stevenson."

His smile evaporated and his entire body locked up.

He'd heard that before. Too often, in fact.

Wes Stevenson, the NFL player. Wes Stevenson, the MVP. Wes Stevenson, the millionaire.

Fuck. He had her all wrong. She wasn't different. She was just like every other honey that wanted to sink her teeth into a pro football player.

He shoved her off of him, making her land hard on the other side of the sofa.

Teegan yelped, throwing her hands out for balance, then shot a look at him. "What the hell's the matter with you?"

Wes was already on his feet, running a hand through his short hair. "Forget it."

"No," she said, her footsteps trailing behind him into the kitchen area.

He bent into the fridge to pull out a beer and cracked it open. He guzzled a large swallow, then finally faced her. "You really had me fooled; you know that?"

Just like his ex. Deceitful, cunning women who only cared about the end result that benefitted them.

"What are you talking about? What did I say?"

"Wes Stevenson?" he said.

She stared with a blank expression. "Yeah, so?"

"I'm a football player," he spat at her.

"Good for you," she threw her words back just as shitty. "You want a cookie now?"

"Quit being cute. You wanna bang me because of what I can do for you."

She looked at him like he had a few screws loose. "Yeah. I'm hoping you can give me an orgasm. Or is that wishful thinking on my part? Tell me now, and I'll lower my standards. But I've been fantasizing about this for a while, so…it's understandable if you can't live up."

He took another swig of beer as he leaned against the wall, bare foot kicked up behind him. "You'd get off; there's no doubt about that. Though the reason is still up for debate."

"I'm not following right now, Wes. Can you just spit it out?"

"Were you planning on running to Juliet after this?" he said. "Once I fucked you? Was that your plan? Rub it in her face that you snared me?"

"What? No! Why would I do that?"

Wasn't that the point anyway? Show Juliet he'd moved on?

"Because you finally got me in bed. You said it yourself; you've fantasized about trapping me. What were you hoping? I'd throw some money or jewelry your way? A parting gift for doing a service for you this weekend? Being your date and fuck partner?"

"If you must know, no. That's not what I had planned. I just couldn't believe that I was going to sleep with you. Someone I've cared about and wanted for so long. But never mind. I don't want to—as you put it—*fuck* someone who thinks I'm doing it to trap him." She turned and started walking toward the bedroom. Over her shoulder, she said, "You have serious unresolved issues, Wes. Not everyone is out to take advantage of you."

"We're not done here." He pushed off the wall to follow with long strides.

"Oh, yes, we are." She ripped her bikini from the headboard and headed toward the bathroom.

He threw out an arm to stop her.

"Get out of my way," she said.

"No."

When she angled pissed-off eyes at him, he said, "I said we're not done here."

Her jaw worked, then, "Fine. If you won't let me change in there…" She tossed her bikini on the mattress, then hooked her fingers into her waistband, dropping her skirt to the ground. Stepping out of it, she grabbed for the hem of her shirt, pulling it up and over her head, leaving her in nothing but a pair of white lace underwear and matching bra. Reaching around her back, her shoulders worked, then her bra unclasped. She pulled it down her arms and tossed it on the bed next to her bathing suit.

Her eyes. He was focusing on her eyes. But the temptation to lower to those round breasts was starting to win out. He needed it. Needed to see them firsthand. Just once.

With a hand on her hip, Teegan flipped her other hand out, palm up. "Well? Speak."

"I...uh...I just thought..."

Tits. He wanted both of them in his mouth right now. At the same time. Equality and all that.

She scoffed and picked up her bikini top. "I don't have time for this." She tied two of the strings together and lifted it to pull down over her head, but Wes was on her in a second. He clenched both her wrists in one hand, keeping her arms in the air.

"Wha-what are you doing?" she asked, her voice husky with desire rather than fear. "Let me go."

"I said we're not done here." Bending, he flicked his tongue over one nipple.

Teegan moaned loudly, then caught herself, squeezing her lips closed.

He grinned. "You like that?"

She turned her chin away. "No."

"You sure?" He returned the favor on the other side.

"Oh, God," she said, strained. "Shit. I—I can't help it."

"Do you want more?"

She stared him down, and he could tell she was trying to stay strong and not give in. Just on principle alone. He gave her a lot of credit. He'd do the same thing.

"Say it, Teegan. If you want it, you need to tell me."

Teegan still wouldn't meet his gaze. "Yes."

"Yes, what?"

She rolled her eyes. "Yes, I want more."

In the span of one nanosecond, Wes swung his other arm under the backs of her legs and dropped her onto the mattress. He fell over her, stomach to stomach, keeping her hands above her head. He pressed his erection against her leg, letting her feel how badly he wanted her, despite how pissed he was at the moment. If this was what she wanted, he'd give it to her. She'd see just how good Wes Stevenson really was.

He kissed between her breasts, then trailed his lips up the column of her neck, stopping under her left ear.

"You smell good," he said. "Like flowers, but not the kind you buy in a store. These are like rich, exotic ones."

"My lotion," she said.

"I approve. Don't stop wearing it this weekend."

"Okay." He felt her nodding as he squeezed her breast, shaping it so her nipple was ripe for sucking.

And suck it he did. Harder and harder until she was writhing beneath him, mumbling a string of sexy nonsense about wanting him inside of her.

"We're nowhere near ready for that yet," he said.

He released her wrists to drop kisses along her stomach, crossing the waistband of her white lace panties. After slipping his tongue into her belly button, eliciting a ragged sigh, he looped his fingers under the fabric and glided them down her legs, tossing them somewhere behind him.

Fuck me.

This was a sight he never would've imagined seeing, not in all his life. Nor would he have imagined enjoying it as much as he did. She was exquisite. Thicker in shape than most of the other women at this wedding, though by no means fat, her body was a complement to his larger frame. She had curves. Beautiful, delicious curves that were going to cradle him through completion. His cock hardened even further, rejoicing in that knowledge.

"You're beautiful," he said, running a hand over the outline of her hip.

"Thank you," she said. "Now show me how beautiful you are."

He laughed from deep in his throat. "Not yet."

Teegan whimpered, so he said, "Soon. Trust me."

Sooner than he wanted, given how rock hard he was.

Pressing her knees open, he settled between them.

"What are you do—"

One slide of his tongue against her, and she bucked against his mouth.

"*Ohhhhh my God!* Yeah, okay. That's amazing."

He did it again.

If he thought her lotion smelled good earlier, it was nothing compared to what Teegan tasted like. Sweet, warm, and ready for him. Gliding a finger into her, he stroked in tandem with his tongue, bringing her right to the edge before slowing his efforts and letting her come back to Earth. Then he'd start back up, listening for her breath to change and feeling her body tense.

He pulled out, hearing her groan in protest before he added a second finger, which awarded him a sweet mewling sound that he wanted to hear on repeat.

Working her harder and faster with his mouth and finger, he waited for that telling sign that she was ready to let go. This time instead of slowing up when she got close, he increased his speed and pressure, earning him a string of *oh Gods*, before he felt her body lock up and her insides tighten around him. He let her ride out her final few waves before he kissed his way back up.

He looked down at her closed eyes, mouth slightly open, and chest rising higher than normal. She had red scrapes along her breasts and neck from his slight stubble. He gently massaged the spots.

Peeking one eye open, she grinned. "That was..." She blew out a breath. "Whoa."

"Hold tight, 'cause we aren't done yet." He got to his feet, stripping off his shirt, shorts, and boxer briefs in record time. He stood above her, deciding which position he wanted to take her from first.

Straight-on missionary. He wanted to look at her beneath him as he drove into her.

Placing a knee between her legs, he hoisted himself onto the bed and froze.

Shit. He didn't bring any condoms with him. The prospect of having sex this weekend had been null and void. And it wasn't like he'd been getting laid during his recovery. He'd avoided the topic altogether for quite a while now. He'd been too pissed off at himself and Juliet to even think about a woman.

Rolling over, he fell onto his back, staring up at the ceiling.

Her face came into view over him. "You giving up already?"

Wes chuckled, a reaction he'd been doing a lot of this weekend, and propped himself on bent elbows. "I don't give up. Ever."

"Then what's the problem? I'm ready; you're ready." She looked straight at his lower half. "You are, aren't you? I mean, he looks like he's pretty ready."

"I'm ready," he said.

"Okay, what gives?"

"You didn't happen to bring any condoms with you to Mexico, did you?"

Her face showed confusion for a second. "No. Why?"

He lifted both eyebrows.

"Oh," she said, her cheeks turning pink.

She mimicked his move and fell hard onto her back on the mattress with a huff. "Guess that means it's a no-go then, huh?"

Wes twisted, throwing an arm across her. "I'm clean."

Her eyes brightened with renewed excitement. "So am I. I had my appointment not long ago. And I'm on the pill."

Perfect. He wanted this so bad.

Play it cool. "I…just this once?"

The few seconds it took Teegan to think about his offer were the longest of his life. He was hard as steel and would do just about anything to be inside her right now.

"Okay," she said. "Just this once."

Thank Christ. He started to lift a leg and hitch it over her—

"But."

"Yeah?" he asked, leg in the air like a dog.

"Let's stop by the gift shop afterward and get a box of condoms," she said. "You know, just in case."

"Deal," he said, getting on top of her, bracing most of his weight on his arms. "How we doin'? You still ready for me?" His fingers found her opening, sliding in with ease. Hell yeah, she was ready. "Teegan," he said, dropping his forehead to hers. "You're going to feel like a fucking dream."

She lifted her hips, rubbing herself against him. "Let's get started, then, shall we?"

He didn't need to be told twice. Gripping his cock, he positioned it where his fingers had just been. And he pressed forward.

With every delicious inch that he climbed, the tighter she gripped him. He didn't want to brag, but he was a big boy. In all areas. And just as he suspected, she cradled and cushioned him perfectly. Better than he'd ever felt.

Her hands went to his back, where she squeezed, her fingernails digging ten imprints into his skin.

Kissing her long and deep, he imitated the motion of his hips with each slide of his tongue. In and out. Intentional. She met him stroke for stroke, wrapping her legs around his waist like a vise.

"I—I—" she mumbled.

"You what?" he said. "Tell me."

"This is so good. So, so good." She pulled his mouth to hers, where she devoured his mouth and tongue, hungry for more. Like she was insatiable.

He understood the feeling.

Shit, he was getting close already. The fact that he hadn't gotten any for a while, plus the tight fit she offered, and the intensity of the moment was driving him over the edge.

But he'd be damned if he fell without her.

"Your turn," he said, wrapping an arm under her, flipping them. He slammed onto his back with her on top of him, their connection still intact.

She froze and blinked rapidly. "Wow."

"Ride me," he said. "Get there. I want you to come apart with me. Do it."

She rested a palm against his chest, rocking her hips once. Her breath hitched, and her eyes closed. She rocked again. Quick exhale, then her features softened.

She was the most amazing sight—complete reverence on her face as she took from him what she wanted.

Her speed increased, sliding up and back at a more frenzied pace. Her eyebrows dipped slightly like she was searching for something. And he knew what she needed. Clenching her ass, he pressed her against him harder, using his strength to drive deeper.

"Oh," she breathed. "Yes," she hissed, "that."

"Come on, Teegan," he said, barely holding on to his own release. "Tell me you're there."

"I'm there. Keep...that."

Another pump and her body locked up.

Yes.

Everything squeezed him to the point of delicious pain. She pulsed around him, and that was all it took before he found his release.

Once they stopped moving, she fell forward, dropping her head on his shoulder. "Holy shit. I needed that really freaking bad."

Wes ran a hand down her hair, gently shifting the loose strands covering her face. He placed a soft kiss on her cheek. "Good."

Teegan picked her head up, smiling. "That was even better than my imagination. I mean, you were...*damn*. You were incredible."

"So were you."

The woman was a man's wet dream. Sweet and thoughtful outside the bedroom, and a complete effing goddess inside of it. He'd never forget the vision of her riding him, taking what she wanted. The passion and single-minded determination she exhibited without censor was something he hadn't experienced with a woman before. That's how sex should be. Raw and open. Both parties connecting in the most elemental and carnal way. Fulfilling one another's needs fully.

Teegan bent an arm over his chest and rested her chin on top of it. "It had absolutely nothing to do with you playing football, you know."

Her comment earlier about who he was.

"I know," he said. "I overreacted. It's a sore subject for me."

"It's understandable, given what happened to you. I've just—" She stopped.

"What?"

"What I said earlier about Misty...it wasn't entirely true."

He glided a few fingers along the smooth skin of her back. "Which part?"

She shivered under his touch. "I care about you. A lot. Misty was right. I've had feelings for you since college. I just never...I never thought it could amount to anything." Then she froze and gazed up at him with alarmed eyes. "Not that I think this means we're together. I know sex is just sex. It doesn't mean we're in a relationship."

The prospect wasn't as unappealing to him as it had been. Truthfully, he was starting to run out of reasons why he and Teegan couldn't be together. Even the long-distance thing didn't seem that farfetched anymore. Plus, if he could have someone in his bed every night who challenged him and met him pump for pump, then all the better.

She suited him. They fit.

There was still the issue of his sister. Jesus, what a mess that would be if he even hinted that this little charade they were pulling had turned real. She'd have Wes's nuts in a clamp so fast he wouldn't know what hit him. CIA torture tactics would seem like a vacation compared to what Misty could cook up.

Teegan was staring at him like she was hoping for an answer, so he said, "Thank you for telling me. We're lying enough to everyone else, the one thing we have between each other is honesty."

Teegan seemed satisfied with that statement because she shifted, holding both sides of his face, and kissed him.

"I think it's time to head to the gift shop now," she said.

Chapter Ten

Wes had leaped from bed, slipped on his shorts, and was at the door faster than Teegan could count to five.

As promised on his way out, he was gone a maximum of ten minutes. Just long enough for Teegan to revel in the pleasant afterglow of their first time together. Her body was languid and content, though not entirely satisfied. She hoped for another round or two before she would get her fill of Wes. He'd unlocked something inside of her—some hidden confidence she'd always hoped to possess, but never dared to reach for.

Wes came back into the room with a huge box of condoms, and the two of them were at it again.

He sat on one of the steps in the private wading pool on their huge balcony, submerged in the water up to his chest. Teegan straddled his lap, taking in the incredible feel of Wes inside of her, the salty air, and the warm breeze across her back and shoulders. Her arms were around his neck, though she didn't have to hold tight. This round was much slower and softer than the first. Each slight move of his body against hers was born out of pure pleasure. Her senses were heightened. Her arousal more potent. It was almost too much. Everything seemed to escalate. Goose bumps erupted along her flesh, though it wasn't because she was cold. It was the overwhelming feeling of bliss.

Wes splayed both hands on her ass, guiding her into the next slide. She willingly followed his lead, exalting each time his breathing changed as he inched back into her. She watched the grooves between his eyebrows deepen with concentration. A light sheen of sweat broke out along his forehead.

"How's this?" he asked in a gentle voice.

"Perfect," she responded.

Teegan brought his mouth to hers, where they kissed slow and deliberate. His tongue finding hers, and not forcing its way in as he'd done before. This time it was a timid touch, like he was asking permission, before he tilted his head and deepened.

It was something out of a dream. The stars glimmered overhead in the night sky, the soft sounds of people in the far-off distance, and faded light of the moon casting a blue glow across Wes's face.

She'd never imagined it could be like this. So beautiful. So powerful.

Then Wes's grip pressed into her skin, his pace starting to increase. He roughly pushed her against him, so she reciprocated by matching his intensity. He groaned, and his eyes squeezed shut. Euphoria overtook her. There was no better feeling than knowing she was causing his reaction. This hard man melted because of what *she* was doing to him.

Her body delighted in that knowledge, making her need for him amplify to epic proportions. They slid against one another at a more hurried pace, the water in the pool making little waves and causing some to cascade over the side. Their tongues stabbed at one another in desperate need. About the time Wes grunted, Teegan's body started to come apart. They rode out their time together, slowly floating back to the present. Her muscles released as she relaxed against him, feeling nothing but an everlasting high.

Wes exhaled, looping her hair behind her ear. "Have I told you yet how much I like our arrangement?"

Chuckling, she said, "I think a time or two, yes."

"Just making sure."

Teegan ran her fingernails through the short hair at Wes's neck, earning her a stomach-flipping growl. "You like that?"

His eyelids lowered, and he nodded, so she moved her hands higher, massaging the back of his scalp.

"Damn, woman," he said, rough. "That feels almost as good as you surrounding me."

"Almost, huh?" She lowered her mouth to his neck, lightly sucking the skin as her fingers continued to caress his head.

He made a sound of approval that immediately had her blood running hot. How that was even possible after two rounds was a mystery, but it was Wes. She was fairly certain she'd never get enough of him.

"Thank you for coming with me," she said.

"It's my job to make a lady come."

She laughed and pulled back to look at him. His eyes had that cute, naughty-boy sparkle and his mouth was curled on one side.

"That as well," she said. "But I meant to the wedding."

"I know, but I like my version better."

"Your version is definitely better," she agreed. "Seriously, though. Thank you."

Wes sobered, gazing at her with a serious expression. "I should thank you. I don't know how I would've gotten through this weekend without your help. You've done everything I asked and then some. You stood by my side even though you knew it wouldn't be easy for you. It takes a special, selfless woman to do that." His knuckles coasted across her cheek, leaving tingles in their wake.

Selfless. That wasn't something she'd envisioned when she'd agreed to this deal, but it sounded like such a compliment when Wes said it. It filled her with joy that he thought of her like that.

"I had to do it," she said. "You deserve to be happy."

"What about you? What do you deserve?"

"Me?" A familiar stir of nerves swirled in her belly, but for once, she ignored them. Told them to take a hike. She didn't need to be that meek woman who couldn't get dates anymore. Tonight, she was a self-assured woman who had pleasured the man of her dreams. Twice.

Trailing a finger across his shoulder muscle, watching as it leaped under her touch, she said, "I'm pretty happy right now."

He smiled wide and bright, seeming satisfied. "How many more times do you think we can make you happy before the weekend is over?"

What about after? a niggling voice in her head kept asking.

She craved to tell him how he'd changed her. How this weekend had been the best of her life. How she wanted it to continue once they left the island.

But she knew her words would be wasted. She'd seen his reaction when Misty suggested Teegan was in love with him. He'd paled, a look of fear crossing his face. He didn't want her beyond this weekend. And no matter how bad she wanted him, it would only hurt to try to convince him. So she put on a brave grin and told him the truth. "I would think at least five. I mean, we have a whole day left, and we really shouldn't let that box of condoms go to waste."

Wes's head fell back as he barked a laugh. "Oh, Teegan," he said. "Why did we wait so long to do this?"

"I don't know," she replied, her heart squeezing. "Guess it just wasn't the right time before."

Or after.

Wes hugged her, which seemed so much more intimate than what they'd just done. She took in the sensation of his naked body clinging to hers. The tight bindings of his arms around her. How comforting it was. How at ease she felt.

How she could stay like this forever. But forever wasn't happening.

She pulled away.

"Hey," he said. "What's wrong?"

"Nothing." She lifted her lips into a cordial expression.

He looked like he wanted to call her bluff, but he didn't. Instead, he kissed her forehead and shifted her onto the step beside him. "Be right back."

She watched him climb out of the pool and head inside toward the bathroom. She hated to gawk, but good Lord he was a beautiful man. Tall, wide, and full of muscle. An earthbound Greek god.

She used the few moments of silence to gather her thoughts. He wasn't hers. He didn't want her. She needed to accept that. No matter how bad it hurt.

When he came back, he placed his foot on the first step to enter the pool. Even in the dimly lit area, the long, white scar across his knee caught her attention.

Of course, she knew it was there, but she hadn't ever seen it up close before. It was at least three inches, maybe four, with dots outlining the outside.

An awkward silence filled their intimate space, so she glanced up to find Wes watching her.

"Yeah, it's pretty gross."

She shrugged. "It's only a scar."

He continued his descent into the water. Once seated, he picked her up and set her across his lap, hands resting on her thigh. "That scar has caused a lot of problems for me."

His eyes took on a glint like he was recalling bad memories. She let him have a moment before she said, "I'm sure. But you overcame them. Think what could've happened if you'd accepted your fate and stayed in that hospital bed without trying to get better. You wouldn't have gotten what you wanted."

He still had a far-off look. "That wasn't an option. I needed to get better. She needed to see me get better."

"She?"

"Juliet," he said. He glanced at Teegan with a grim laugh. "I believed that if I fully healed she'd want me. She'd come back."

"That's why you did it? Pushed yourself so hard in physical therapy? To get Juliet back?"

He was nodding, staring in the direction of the ocean.

Did football have anything to do with his recovery at all? Did he still want to play? Or was it only Juliet? A driving desire to win her back because he knew she wanted him to play. And now that he was going back into the NFL, what did that mean for Wes and Juliet? Was he still hoping she'd want him back?

Teegan didn't have a chance to ask because Wes lifted his hand to look at his watch. "The rehearsal dinner is going to start soon. I don't want to move from this spot, but we should go. Otherwise, people will talk."

People? Or person?

"Yeah," she said, standing. "We don't want the bride getting upset."

His eyebrows lowered, but she didn't give him time to question her statement.

"I'm going to hop in the shower." She got up and let him watch her walk away naked.

And all she could think was: when was the revenge he talked about going to happen?

Chapter Eleven

It was nine at night but given the brightly lit floating orbs in the pool, the illuminated tiki torches lining the gardens, and the numerous candles on surrounding tables, Teegan easily maneuvered to the bar without the risk of tripping and falling in front of the entire wedding party.

Lighting aside, her wobbly legs were something else entirely. Wes touched her like she mattered. Like she meant something to him. But then he said those things about Juliet, and it confused Teegan to no end. Did he want his ex back?

Teegan felt a much stronger tie to Wes now. One that sent a fissure of worry through her. How was she going to walk away and act as if nothing happened between them? How could she watch him on the field and pretend those hands of his hadn't touched every part of her body?

And another woman…how would she accept him dating again? What if it ended up being Juliet? She was getting married, but nothing was a done deal until she said I do. Right?

Ignore it. Enjoy the time you have left.

She stopped at a private cabana by the pool, where Jessica and Avery reclined on lounge chairs, sipping pink drinks in tall glasses.

Jessica was in a navy sundress with gold embroidery down the front, and her long, lean legs stretched out in front of her. "Where the hell have you been, you slut?"

Teegan sucked in a breath. Did they know?

Oh, right. Yeah, they thought she was getting it on the regular from Wes, not for the first time tonight. She relaxed, choosing a seat at Jessica's feet on the end of the cushioned lounge chair.

"I think you know where I was," she said, letting her tone confirm Jessica's assumption.

"Seriously?" Jessica said. "I hate you right now!"

"Oh, stop." Amused, Avery leaned to her right to lightly smack Jessica on the shoulder. Her dress was similar in cut to Jess's, hitting mid-thigh and tailored at her trim waist, except it was splashed with a pattern of white, bright pink, and green palm trees. "Don't make her feel bad for getting some. If we all could be so lucky this week."

"I second that," Saylor said, making her way to where the other women sat. Lowering onto the end of Avery's chair, Saylor folded her hands in her lap over her all-white ensemble. "Dave has done nothing but play golf this entire weekend. And then at night, he tells me he's too tired to do anything but lie there."

"I heard something similar from Ian last night." Jessica made a scoffing sound through tight lips. "Men. What kind of golf are they playing? Triathlon style?"

"Please," Avery said. "They don't even have to walk this course. They spent the extra money to reserve golf carts. Lazy bastards."

Jessica and Saylor lifted their drinks in salute.

Teegan chuckled, mostly because she didn't have any reason to complain. Her lady parts were more than happy. It was her heart that was a bit tangled at the moment.

Jessica was looking out past the pool toward a large, wooden pergola. It was bare right now, but they'd been told it would be filled with flowers and white drapery for the wedding. The hotel staff was starting to bring out white Chiavari chairs and lining them to face the makeshift altar. The crystal blue water, though not visible in the dark, would serve as a gorgeous backdrop for the ceremony.

Under the archway stood Juliet and LJ. They faced one another, holding hands, while the priest walked them through the sequence of events for the wedding.

"Think they'll go through with it?" Jessica asked, staring at the couple.

Avery smacked her again.

"What?" Jessica asked. "It's a legit question. Juliet isn't exactly known for staying with one guy forever." She slid a look at Teegan that seemed to say, *Thankfully*.

It was true. If Juliet hadn't left Wes when he was down and out, he wouldn't be here right now with Teegan. Teegan would probably be attending *their* wedding. Oh, and let's not forget that Teegan wouldn't have had those mind-blowing orgasms, either. What a shame that would've been.

Just the thought of sex with Wes made her insides clench like greedy nymphos.

Yeah, she hoped there was more time between the sheets in store for them tonight. A fireworks display of massive proportions. A final, unforgettable farewell.

"I think she'll go through with it," Teegan said.

Attention from all three women swung her way in varying degrees of expression.

"You do?" Avery said with eyebrows lifted. "Why? What makes you say that?"

Teegan shrugged. "She's getting what she wants. A rich NFL player who adores her and buys her whatever she wants."

"You think that's all it is?" Saylor asked. "Do you think she even loves him?"

They turned back to watching the couple, who were now looking into each other's eyes adoringly.

"Seems like she does," Avery said. "But who knows? She supposedly loved Wes too."

"True."

Everyone nodded in agreement.

"I don't know," Jessica said. "There was always something about her and Wes. They fit. I still can't believe she did that to him."

Teegan swallowed down the jealousy rising from her friend's comment. She knew Jess didn't mean anything by it, nothing malicious at least. They'd all thought Juliet and Wes had been a match made in heaven.

Teegan thought back to what Wes had said earlier in their room. How angry he'd been.

"Were you planning on running to Juliet after this?" he'd said. "Once I fucked you? Was that your plan? Rub it in her face that you snared me?"

Was he angry because he thought Teegan was like Juliet? Or because he was afraid Juliet wouldn't want him after finding out he'd been with Teegan?

The woman he'd loved had used him, and he was obviously still wary about trusting anyone else. Especially now that he was planning to play pro football again. There would be plenty of people who would want a piece of him.

But Teegan didn't want him because of his fame.

She wanted him. Wes Stevenson the man. Not the football player. Not the athletic company spokesperson. Not even Misty's brother. Just him. The way he made her feel. Alive. Confident. Sexy.

"It was surprising," Saylor said in her sweet, Southern accent. "I never took Juliet as someone who could do that to a person she loved. She walked out when he needed her most. I couldn't imagine doing that to David."

Avery and Jessica nodded their heads, mumbling their agreement.

"Me either," Teegan said, meaning it. She'd hated hearing from Misty how miserable and hurt Wes had been when Juliet left. Everything he loved had been taken away without being able to do anything to stop it. He must have felt so helpless.

Jessica nudged Teegan with her gold-sandaled foot. "At least you don't have to worry about that. He's yours now."

"I'm so glad he has someone like you, Tee," Avery chimed in. "He deserves a good woman who will love him for the right reasons."

"Yeah," Teegan said. He did deserve it. Too bad she wasn't going to be that woman.

You won't know for sure unless you ask him.

True. She'd wimped out earlier.

Tonight. She'd ask him tonight. After she'd had her fill one last time.

Images of their lovemaking immediately exploded in her mind. A flood of warmth filled her. Their clothes falling to the floor. His hands trailing down her body. His—

"Oh my God!" Jessica said, nudging Teegan a little harder with her foot. "Stop that!"

"Stop what?"

"I can see your face. You're totally thinking about doing him right now. Have mercy on the rest of us, will ya? Not all of us are going back to our rooms with a professional sports player."

Teegan placed a straight arm behind her and leaned back on it. "Do me a favor and stop saying that, okay?"

"What? The sports player thing?"

Teegan nodded. "He's sensitive about it. Wouldn't you be if your fiancée left you because you couldn't play anymore?"

The ladies didn't say anything for a moment, then Jessica looked back to where Juliet and LJ stood more casually; the rehearsal seemed to be wrapping up. "Man, I wish Wes's injury hadn't been that bad."

"Why?" Teegan asked. "What do you mean?"

"I wish he could play again, so he could crap in Juliet's face and make her regret walking away from him."

"You think she'd care now that she's marrying LJ, who is a football player too?" Saylor asked.

"Oh, she'd care," Jess said. "It's Wes. LJ is the first runner-up. I guarantee if Wes were able to play, she'd be on him so fast, LJ wouldn't know what hit him."

"You-you do?" Teegan tripped over her tongue, her throat suddenly dry as the sand under her feet.

Jessica placed her empty glass on the table to her right, and curled her legs under her, resting on her hip. "Hell yeah. If she left him because he couldn't play anymore, then she'd sure as shit try to get him back if he could."

Teegan had raised her glass to finish the final sip, but she found that she suddenly lost interest in the delicious fruity cocktail. She glanced down at it, twisting the stem slightly between index finger and thumb. "Yeah, I guess you're right."

He came down here for revenge, but what if the possibility was real that he could have his ex back? He wanted to come because Juliet was getting married. What if she wasn't anymore? What if she made herself available to him? Would he consider the possibility? They had such a long history together. As Jessica said, they fit. Everyone knew that.

"You okay?" Avery asked. "You got quiet all of a sudden."

Teegan popped her head up and attempted a smile. "I'm good. Just thinking about the future."

Jessica stretched an arm over her head and sighed. "And what a bright, deliciously hot one it'll be for you, my dear."

• • •

Teegan thought about what the women said as she kept an eye out for Wes. He'd been catching up with his teammates while she was talking with Jess, Avery, and Saylor. He and Jamal had paired off, laughing with one another by the bar.

Sights set on the buffet line, Teegan headed that way but was intercepted by Juliet.

"Hey there," she said, stopping at Teegan's side. "How are you?"

"Good." Teegan glanced around, confused why Juliet was talking with her. She'd assumed they'd avoid each other most of the weekend since, you know, Teegan brought her hot ex to her wedding. "Uh, good."

"Are you having fun?"

"Yes," Teegan said, a few moments sticking out more than others this weekend. Most—okay, *all*—had been behind closed doors with Wes.

"Good. That's good." Juliet looked at her like her brain was working millions of light years a second. "I'm thrilled you could come."

"Me too. Thanks for the invite."

"And thanks for Wes," she said like Teegan hadn't just spoken. "I'm glad you were able to bring him. It's been ages since we've been able to catch up. He looks well."

"Sure," Teegan said, suddenly on guard at the mention of her date. It was the way Juliet said it with her eyes a little too perky and her smile a little too wide. "He is well. He's doing awesome. We're happy."

Juliet's smile turned a little devious, and her bright eyes sharpened, but Teegan ignored it. Or she tried to. She was probably imagining it.

"So, the wedding," Teegan said, glancing out over the elaborate pink and white decorations scattered over the tables and chairs. "It's going to be pretty."

Juliet didn't follow her gaze, choosing instead to stay focused on Teegan. "How long have you and Wes been together anyway?"

The shock of her question was enough to make Teegan's throat close up. "We, uh, well, we've been together a while."

"What's a while?"

"You know, like, a few months."

"Hmm," Juliet said. "That's interesting because Wes said it's only been a few weeks."

Teegan thrust a laugh out, trying to play it off. "Weeks. Months. Who knows? You know how men are. They don't remember anniversaries unless we women remind them. Am I right?"

Juliet tipped her head to the side slightly. "No. Wes remembered every important date we ever had. Birthdays. Anniversaries. He was fantastic with things like that. It's a shame he can't recall yours." Her face looked like she wanted to show pity, but she wasn't even close. Instead, it bordered satisfaction.

"Yeah, well. We revel in the everyday. Not only the important days."

That knocked Juliet's smirk down a notch.

"And besides," Teegan went on, "when you're doing it as often as we are, hours and hours on end, it's hard to keep track of one day from the next."

Juliet's mouth opened and then her top lip lifted like she was doing an Elvis impression. "It's easy to get wrapped up in the excitement and sexual attraction. Wes is incredible for sure, but what about the everyday?"

"What about it?"

"Aren't you tired of sitting around listening to him complain about his career and his crushed dreams? He was so incessant about it."

"Nope," Teegan said. "He's doing great physically. You'd barely know his knee was busted however long ago. He gets around on it extremely well."

"I've noticed." Juliet's eyes found Wes on the other side of the gathering. He was watching them, seeming to take a keen interest. "It's too bad he isn't playing anymore. He was the perfect guy."

Anger bubbled up. "Was?"

Juliet brought her wistful expression back to Teegan. "Amazing body. Thoughtful attitude. And so many endorsement deals. The money he made was ridiculous, and he only had to be out of the house a few times a year. It was perfect."

Teegan's lips twisted. "You talk about him like he's a prize horse or something."

Juliet turned her striking blue eyes on Teegan. "Isn't he?"

"No. He's a person. A living, breathing man who has a heart and feelings."

Juliet grinned, showing her straight, white teeth. "Come on, Tee. You might have everyone else fooled, but I know better."

"What are you talking about? Know better about what?"

"You'll learn soon enough." And Juliet turned around and walked away.

Wes passed Juliet on his way toward Teegan. The other woman smiled at him and glided a hand across his shoulder, ramping Teegan's jealousy up even further.

"What was that all about?" he asked Teegan.

She watched Juliet's hips sway behind the fabric of her form-fitting dress. "No clue. But she made it clear that you'd be the perfect guy if you were playing football."

His eyes hardened as the muscles in his jaw ticked. "Did she now?"

"Yep." And for curiosity sake, Teegan decided to take it a step further, to see what he would say. "She made it seem like if you were playing again, she'd try to get you back."

A flash of surprise raced across his features. "She said that?"

Teegan lifted her shoulders. "Not in those exact words, but yeah. What do you think about that? Would you want her back?"

Wes didn't answer her question. He just stood, watching Juliet and LJ in each other's arms, his jaw still working.

Teegan placed her hand on his arm, grabbing his attention back.

She studied his face, trying her hardest to discern any meaning from it. He'd been so stoic when they'd first arrived at the resort. So determined. Then with each passing day, he'd seemed to mellow. He was now laughing and joking with his teammates. Conversing pleasantly with Juliet's family. Fitting right back into this scene so naturally.

Had the few days spent around Juliet made him remember their good times together? Had he forgiven her?

Teegan didn't want to know the answer because she feared he had.

And what scared her most was that he did want Juliet back.

Chapter Twelve

Wes filling her was a sensation she was never going to get tired of. Even if they never saw each other after this moment, even if he wanted Juliet back, there was something so supremely enjoyable about the way only he touched her. The trail of his slightly roughened fingers down her cheek. The exquisite pull of his mouth against her nipple. The way that, despite his size, she still knew he wouldn't hurt her.

They'd always have this. Their time here in Mexico.

Wes was on top of Teegan, holding a majority of his weight on his bent elbows as he rocked into her. She wanted all of Wes, raw and wild, so she could remember this moment for as long as she needed to. It was going to hurt like a bitch if he didn't want her after this weekend, so she was taking from him what she could while she had the chance.

His mouth was at her ear, labored breaths pelting against her sensitive skin. Pulling back, he held her cheek with one hand and kissed her long and deep, their tongues dancing to the rhythm their bodies had set.

Both of Teegan's hands were on his back, holding tight to keep purchase so she could encourage him where she needed. She wanted to grip his ass in the worst way, but her arms just simply weren't long enough to reach. Wes, on the other hand, had no trouble reaching hers. She could always tell when he was getting close because he would glide his large palm down her side and dip it beneath her to prop her into a higher angle. Which worked in increasing her approach to release too. Within seconds, his rapid heartbeat pounded against her chest, her own heart trying to leap out and meet his. She felt the peak of her orgasm starting to take hold just as his stomach sucked in.

"Find it," he said in a ragged voice. "Come on, Teegan. I'm right there."

She hastened the motion of her hips, skin slapping against skin, to reach the end. It was building, growing to the point it was almost agonizing. The struggle, the anticipation, the utter disappointment that this was likely it for them. She squeezed her eyes closed, concentrating on nothing but savoring this moment.

He met her stroke for stroke before he groaned on an exhale just as everything inside of her squeezed tight and blew apart. She grunted her release, not feeling the least bit embarrassed by the unladylike reaction. It was a satisfying end that continued to pulse through her for a few seconds more.

Wes rolled off her with a hand propping his head up. She placed her head on his shoulder, threw a bent leg across him, and circled his large pecs with light grazes of her fingers.

"That tickles," he said, bringing her hand up to kiss the inside of her wrist.

Her heart melted at the sweet gesture. How wonderful would it be to stay like this forever? Or maybe not forever, but for a good, long while. Enough time that she could show him that he was deserving of love and attention for the right reasons.

"Wes," she said. "I love sharing this with you."

He made an approving sound. "Me, too."

"You know," she went on, "I was thinking."

"Yeah? 'Bout what? If you want to go again, I need at least another thirty minutes."

She laughed. "That wasn't it, but that's good to know. Tell him to start gearing up; the clock starts now."

He took hold of her thigh and hoisted it higher across him,

caressing. Up and down. Soft and slow.

"What if we kept this thing going?" she asked breathily. "Like, after this weekend."

His fingers froze on her thigh, and he didn't say anything.

"I—I mean, I know that's not what we agreed, but I just thought…we get along. And the sex is…the sex is great, and well, I wouldn't mind doing it more. And seeing you more. If you're up for it, that is."

His hand disappeared from her leg, making her feel cold in an instant.

He pressed her chin up so she could look at him. When she did, he sighed. "Teegan, we agreed. This is it. This is all it can be."

"I know, but—"

"Don't get me wrong. I love being like this with you. Sleeping with you is more than I could've imagined."

Okay, that was something.

"But, you have a life in New York, mine's in Houston."

"I know, but—"

"And Misty would freak if she found out I was naked with you right now, let alone going home with you."

"Yeah, but—"

"And I've got football to think about," he said. "It's going to be hard enough to make a comeback. I need my head clear if I'm going to do this. I can't afford to have any distractions."

"Oh," she said, emptiness starting to replace the glow she'd just felt. "Right. Yeah. It's not you, it's me, right?"

The one man she finds who makes her feel like she can conquer the world, and he chooses his career.

What about Juliet? Ask him about Juliet.

"Come on, Teegan. Don't look at me that way. I'm trying to do the best I can right now. This is all new for me. The last time I went through this, I was already with someone. But I think trying to get back on the field and start a relationship would be hard to do. At least, successfully. One would have to suffer."

His tone alluded that football wouldn't be the one. Of course, it wouldn't. It's all he'd wanted for a year. It's all he'd thought about. He was going to put 200 percent into it. Which meant that any attempt they'd make together wouldn't be much time at all. He'd be solely focused on football. "What about Juliet?"

His face hardened. "What about her?"

"How does she fit into this equation?"

"I don't know what you mean."

"What if she wasn't getting married?"

"What?"

"Would you want her?" she asked, wondering where all this awesome confidence was coming from.

"N-no," he said. "Why would you ask that?"

"It's why you worked so hard at therapy, wasn't it? Didn't you say you did it for her?"

"At first, yeah, but—"

"But then she got with LJ, and you figured you'd have to fight to win her back?"

"Yes. No. You're confusing things, Teegan."

"Am I?" she asked. "What would make it simpler for you? Me stepping aside and letting her have you?"

He sat up a bit. "You and I aren't together, so there's nowhere for you to step."

"Conveniently," she said, pulling away from him.

"What's gotten into you?"

"I don't know. Probably a man who's just passing the time until someone better comes along."

Wes didn't say anything, but he searched her face. For what she didn't know.

"You know what?" he said. "I need some air." He got out of bed and grabbed his shorts, slipping into them. He reached for the ice bucket on the side table. "I'm gonna go fill this up. While I'm gone, why don't you order some food? Then maybe by the time I get back, we can have a real conversation like adults."

"Sure," she said, yanking the covers up to her neck. Covering one's breasts seemed like the right thing to do when arguing.

He took in the move, shaking his head before spinning toward the door. He hustled out, as it slammed closed.

Teegan glanced around the room, feeling the loss of Wes immediately. That quick she regretted her decision to bring up Juliet. But she had to know.

Room service was the last thing she should be concerned about right now, but he'd said order food, and she was starting to get a bit hungry, so she reached beside the bed for the menu. Glancing at the variety of food, she dialed the number and ordered a ton of different things ranging from steak, grilled cheese, vegetable soup, Mediterranean salad, pizza, and two containers of ice cream. Eh, he was a big guy. Plus, it was charging to the room with his credit card. At the moment, she didn't feel bad about that. And he had the money to cover it.

After hanging up, she ventured into the bathroom and grabbed the robe hanging on the back of the door. She went back to her lounged position, covered up, preparing for their next battle. Footsteps and voices sounded outside her door, and she kept waiting for the unmistakable sound of the door latching open.

Twenty minutes or so passed and still no Wes. She was starting to get worried.

Then a knock hit the door.

Getting up, she checked the peephole, seeing a dark-haired woman in a hotel uniform with a tray on the other side.

She opened, and with a sweep of her arm, welcomed the woman in. "You can set the trays there." Teegan pointed to a spot on the desk by the balcony where the ice bucket had been.

The woman latched something on the door to keep it open and wheeled the tray inside. She lifted the lids of the food containers, making Teegan's stomach go nuts with the amazing smells.

Teegan heard an odd sound. A giggle. Then she could have sworn she heard Wes's voice. It was low as if it was nearby.

"I'll be right back," she said to the other woman, who looked at Teegan like she'd asked her to jump off the balcony.

She traveled a few steps in the direction the sounds came from, about thirty paces down the hall.

Wes's naked back came into view, giving her heart a bit of a start. She'd seen it, grabbed it, licked it, and kissed it, but the sight still seemed fresh and new. Sure, she was pissed at him, but come on, the man had a hot-ass body.

She went a few more steps. His entire backside came into view, but she couldn't see his face past the corner of the wall where the ice machine was nestled. A few more steps, then a pair of hands came around his neck. And a head. There was a blond head planted against his, connected by their lips.

Juliet.

Oh my God, Wes and Juliet are kissing by the ice machine!

Juliet let out a purring sound that made Teegan's stomach turn.

Teegan jumped back, not processing what she saw. Revenge. Wes had wanted revenge on Juliet. Not a make-out session. So why was he kissing her?

Well, you did ask him if he wanted her back. Maybe he's testing the waters to give you an answer.

"Ma'am?"

Teegan spun to see the woman who brought room service with her head out the door of Teegan's room. She waved a flat, black rectangle in the air.

Not sure what the hell to do at the moment, Teegan sprinted down the hall, her brain a frazzled mess. "Sorry."

The hotel employee handed Teegan the bill holder with the

receipt inside. Teegan reviewed the order, making sure everything she'd ordered was on there.

"How's your night going?" she asked.

"Good, thank you," the hotel employee said with a heavy Spanish accent. "Yours?"

"Eh, could be better." Teegan glanced up at her. "What's your name?"

"Amarosa."

"Nice to meet you. I'm Teegan. You have a boyfriend? Husband? Some kind of man in your life, Amarosa?"

The woman shook her head. "He left us a few years ago."

"Us?"

"Me and my son. He's seven."

"Hmm," Teegan said. "Men are like that, aren't they? Let you believe they're into you, that you're the only woman, and then—*BAM*—they up and leave."

Amarosa's eyes widened, but she nodded. "I guess so."

"What's your son's name?"

"Xavier."

Teegan looked down at the tip line and placed the end of the ballpoint pen on it. "He ever been to Disney World? Your son?"

"No, ma'am," Amarosa said in a confused tone.

"Well," Teegan said. "Tell him you're going to take him."

"Excuse me?" Amarosa said.

Teegan wrote a two with three zeros behind it for the tip, then signed the bill, and handed it back with the folio open.

Amarosa looked down, her eyes focusing on what Teegan had written, and she squealed. "*Oh, dios mio! Gracias!*" She hugged Teegan hard enough to knock the wind out of her.

"You're welcome," she said, struggling for air.

Amarosa exited the same time Wes was walking in.

He did a double take, obviously noticing the other woman's excited gait. "What's up with her?"

Teegan dropped her gaze to the ice cream she was pulling the lid off of. "Just really loves her job, I guess."

He sidled up next to her, standing close enough that her body should've thrummed with excitement. Not this time. Not after what she'd just witnessed. Though it did hum pretty hard with the enjoyment of giving his money away.

"Looks like you got a good mix of food," he said, scanning the table. "Thanks. I'm starving."

She scooped a huge helping of ice cream onto a spoon and put it into her mouth. Through full cheeks that were now burning from the cold, she gave him a half-assed, closed-lip smile. "Enjoy," she mumbled making ice cream drizzle out of the side of her mouth.

His eyebrows scrunched. "You okay?"

Shrugging, she turned away. "Sure. All good."

Depositing herself on the bed, she proceeded to devour Ben and Jerry like their cream was the most delicious thing she'd ever tasted. Right now, it was. There was no way the other man in this room was getting his cream anywhere near her mouth tonight. Not after his lips were on Juliet. Teegan wasn't anyone's sloppy seconds. Or was it thirds? Teegan already had sex with Wes, then he kissed Juliet, which made Juliet the sloppy seconds, then he'd be coming back to Teegan, making her third.

You know what? Forget it. She was done with this. Wes and Juliet could have a nice, long, happy life together endorsing expensive running shoes. Teegan didn't like working out anyway.

She shot up from the bed, passing right by him, en route to the bathroom. She closed the door and locked it behind her, then set the ice cream on the marble counter. She unfastened the robe and dropped it onto the floor, then donned her favorite worn-out Yankees T-shirt and NYU boxer shorts. Picking the pint back up—as if she'd leave that here in this room for him to eat—she stomped out of the bathroom and slipped into her flip-flops.

"I'll be back for my things in the morning," she said and headed toward the door.

His footsteps were right behind her. "Hold up. Where are you going?"

"To another room."

She reached for the handle and yanked it toward her, but a strong arm slammed the door shut. Without facing him, she growled, "Let me out."

"Not until you tell me what's gotten into you."

Teegan whirled on him. "Into me? How about what's gotten into you?"

"What are you talking about?"

"Where's the ice bucket Wes?" Her anger level was spiking high enough to blur her vision. "Forget about it while you had your lips all over Juliet?"

He drew back, surprise blanketing his features as he glanced down at his empty hands. "That—that was—"

"That—that was," she mocked his tone. Then she got up into his face, or the best she could at her height. "Did you even come for revenge? Or was this your plan all along? Beg me to bring you so that you could get a backstage pass for a meet and greet with the bride?"

"What? No!"

"What, then?" She slapped a hand onto his abs and tried to give him a hearty shove. "Do you still want her? That it?"

"Yes!" he shouted back, regaining his balance.

It was as if Teegan had been struck. With what she didn't know. His hand. A baseball bat. Nine thousand volts of electricity. It all would've hurt exactly the same.

Then almost as if he was surprised by his response, he quickly said, "No." He ran a hand over his short hair. "Fuck. I don't know, okay?"

"Wrong answer," Teegan said with a shake of her head.

"Thanks for a fantastic weekend and for being a stellar date. This is definitely one for the history books."

"You're mad at me now?"

"You're just now catching on? Man, I knew you jocks were dumb and all, but this reaches a whole new level."

He seemed to grow a few inches taller in that moment. He towered over her like a menacing shadow. "You brought me to this wedding knowing my intentions. I didn't lie to you or hide the fact that I wanted to get back at Juliet."

"Oh, yeah, that tongue down her throat really showed her who's boss."

"Would you let the kiss go for one goddamn second?"

"No," she said. "Because you obviously have unresolved feelings for your ex."

"So?"

"*So?*" she replied with a wicked laugh. "You came to the wedding with me!"

He bent and got right up into her face. "Because I had to! Not because I wanted to!"

They were both breathing heavy now, chests heaving, staring each other down as if they wanted to catch the other one on fire. Poof. Up in flames.

She stepped back, digging her spoon into the now soft ice cream. Bastard. He'd distracted her so long that her ice cream had melted. She hated melted ice cream.

Getting a nice big glob onto her spoon, she twisted her wrist around and flung it at him. It landed exactly where she'd aimed— across his left eye and cheek.

His face heated so fast and so hot that the ice cream liquefied almost immediately. It ran down his face in a thick, white trail. He swiped at it, leaving a smear across his cheek.

"You shouldn't have done that." He stepped forward, reaching for her.

Teegan yelped, released the pint and spoon, causing them to fall and splatter onto the carpet as she whipped around and ran for the door. She got it open and was almost through when an arm the width of a tree trunk jerked her back. She slammed into Wes's rock-hard chest, and his arm held her there like a steel clamp. She watched as the door closed with a resounding slam.

His mouth was at her ear. "I had other plans for that ice cream, so I don't appreciate you wasting it."

"Yeah?" she said. "What kind of plans?" She could already tell what he meant by his tone, but apparently, she was a masochist and had to hear it.

"I was going to smear it across you—" His arm shifted so he could keep a hold on her but also grip one of her breasts in his large, rough palm. It was torture. "—and let it melt down your body so I could lick it off...all the way down..." His other hand slid past the elastic of her shorts to cup her between her legs.

Oh, good God. She quivered at his touch, and she knew he felt it because his lips curled against her cheek.

"See what you'd miss if you leave?"

"Better to walk out and save my dignity, then spend another minute with a man who doesn't want me."

Hardness pressed against her butt. "Does that feel like I don't want you?"

"In all the ways but the one that matters," she said.

His arms immediately loosened. He didn't attempt to keep her against him as she stepped out of his hold and turned to face him.

"I deserve to be loved, Wes. All the way. Not by someone who wants to sleep with me when it suits him, but by someone who accepts every piece of me. Which guy are you?"

Come on. Be the right guy. Be him. I want you to be him.

He didn't say anything right away, but she could tell his mind was working. Probably trying to figure out the best way to let her down easy.

He must have come to some conclusion because his shoulders lowered. "Teegan."

Her heart sank. Yeah, she wasn't waiting around to hear some lame-ass excuse why she was a great woman but wasn't great enough.

Her eyes closed momentarily, mostly so she didn't have to look at his pleading expression.

"We made a deal," he started.

"Save it," she said. "I'll see you tomorrow at the wedding. Good night, Wes."

She opened her eyes and stepped to the door. No footsteps behind her this time.

Teegan opened the door, walked through, and made her way down the hall toward Jessica's room. Or Avery's. Or Saylor's. But definitely not Misty's. Teegan would prefer to live until morning, and that wouldn't happen if Misty heard about everything that transpired between her and Wes over the last twenty-four hours.

• • •

Wes stood on the other side of his sister's door, bolstering his courage to knock.

Just do it. Get it over with.

He didn't have a clue where Teegan went, but he figured he'd start with Misty. She was Teegan's best friend and the person she confided in most.

He needed to find Teegan and tell her how he felt. After she'd left, he realized what an idiot he'd been. When she'd asked him if he was that guy—the guy she needed—his insides seized momentarily. He'd completely rejected the question. He'd convinced himself that he was better off with no one. It was football and football alone that would keep him company. It's all he'd wanted. Especially after Juliet.

But…somewhere between Teegan walking out and him standing in that empty suite, he realized he wanted football and Teegan.

Or just Teegan. And what a revelation that was. He'd been busting his ass for more than a year, getting into tip-top shape to play in the NFL again, and he realized that it didn't matter. He'd give it all up tomorrow if he could have Teegan.

But who knew if she'd even accept him now.

He'd kissed Juliet. There was no denying that. Their lips touched, and her arms had been around his neck. It felt okay. For about a second, before his brain registered what was happening. He'd wanted Juliet for so long. He'd craved for things to go back to the way they'd been before his accident.

But that was before he'd fallen in love with Teegan.

Wes was ready to do nearly anything to prove it.

He needed to find her.

Stiffening his spine, he lifted his fist and banged on the door.

Rustling sounded on the other side, a loud bang like someone fell out of bed, then a, "Damn it. Shit. Christ." Heavy footsteps approached.

"Who is it?" came Misty's strained voice.

"It's me, sis," he said.

"It's fine, Jim. It's just Wes," she said as the door clicked open.

Not sure why it mattered who it was on the other side, but with these two, who knew.

The door swung open to reveal Misty in a brown button-up shirt, baggy shorts with cargo pockets, and a gun belt with a revolver in the holster. She held a riding crop in her right hand.

He looked her over. "What the hell are you supposed to be? You look like a homeless Indiana Jones."

"Rick Grimes," she said as if that helped.

"Who?"

Misty rolled her eyes. "*The Walking Dead*?"

"The show?"

"Yes, the show, you dimwit. What else would it be?"

"I have no idea."

She blew out an aggravated breath. "I'm busy. What do you want?"

"Teegan," he said. "Is she here?"

"I sure as hell hope not."

"What does that mean?"

"You don't want to know." The way her eyes filled with unconcealed exhilaration told him she was absolutely right.

"Forget it," he said. "Do you know where she might be?"

Misty placed her free hand on her hip and glared at him. "Why isn't she with you?"

He hesitated, trying to frame it the right way.

The riding crop sliced across his right arm.

"Ow!" he howled. "Shit!"

"Speak."

"She...she and I..."

Smack. She hit him again.

He cringed back, rubbing the sting from his arm. "That really freakin' hurts, you know."

"You're wasting my time. Tell me what happened or the next one is hitting you somewhere else." Her gaze lowered below his belt, so he found his words real quick.

"I fucked up," he said.

"I gathered that," Misty said. "How bad?"

"Bad. She caught Juliet and me kissing."

Misty chewed on the inside of her cheek, which was a blessing since she didn't immediately smack him again. Then she waved her finger in a come-here gesture. He bent and brought his face close to hers so she could tell him what would make this right. Instead, she slapped him across the back of the head with her open palm. Hard. It stung like a bitch and his ears rang.

"You're an idiot," she said, straightening.

"Yeah, we've established that." He massaged away the pain pulsing in his head. "How do I fix it?"

She crossed her arms. "Just so we're clear. What does fix it mean?"

"I want to make it up to Teegan. I need her. I want her." He swallowed the enormous lump in his throat that his admission caused. "Like, want her, want her. Forever."

He wasn't sure his sister had overcome her aversion to her friends dating her brother. But he didn't care. Ever since Teegan walked out, he had this hole in his chest that seemed to grow deeper the longer he was separated from her. He knew the only way to fill it was to wrap her in his arms and never let her go.

Her stoic expression didn't budge. "And she wants you?"

He shifted his weight onto both feet. Did she? He thought she did. At least until his lips had stupidly touched Juliet's. "I think so. She asked me if I could be *the guy*."

"Well?" she said, propping a hand on her hip. "Can you? Are you?"

"I—I wanna be. I—"

She raised the riding crop above her shoulder.

"Yes!" He cowered. "Yes, okay? I can! I can! I will be!"

Seeming satisfied, Misty lowered the torture device and gave him an evil smile.

"So?" he said. "How do I fix it?"

"Hell if I know."

His heart deflated. "Why am I here then?"

She shrugged. "Beats me."

"Babe?" Jim called from inside the room. "This makeup is starting to itch my face. I think I'm allergic."

"You're fine," she called over her shoulder. "Just keep it on a few more minutes. I want to act out that scene at the carnival where Michonne thinks Rick was eaten alive by the zombies, but instead, they were chowing down on a deer. Only you're going to chow down on me." She looked at Wes and lowered her voice. "He's the zombie this time."

Oh, for fuck's sake. Wes's stomach churned. "Do you have to talk about that while I'm standing here?"

"You interrupted us, remember? We have one night left. We're making the most of it."

"Seriously," Jim said in a high-pitched voice. "Hon, it's burning!"

Misty groaned. "I gotta get back in there before he breaks character."

"Anything?" Wes asked. "Can you tell me anything that might help?"

"She doesn't give a shit about football or your money. If you're going to win her back, prove to her that you care about her. That you want her. Not some Juliet stand-in."

"But I don't want some Juliet stand-in."

"Does Teegan know that? I'm guessing not if she left you so easily."

Chapter Thirteen

When Teegan left last night, she went to the front desk and asked for a room. They still had her information from her previous reservation that Wes had upgraded, so she asked the hotel to charge her for any room they could find. It ended up being on the other side of the resort. A much smaller, much simpler space, which was fine by her. She was only using it to sleep.

Though not much sleeping happened. Between tossing and turning, the rest of the night was spent reliving Juliet and Wes's kiss in vivid detail. The sickness in her stomach wouldn't subside.

She'd finally given up and headed out the door around five thirty. She was sitting at the resort café, staring out at the blue ocean as she sipped her second mimosa when Jessica approached out of breath.

Jess lowered into the seat across from Teegan, her ample chest heaving beneath a slim-fitting blue yoga tank. Her black hair was gathered into a smooth ponytail that trailed down between her shoulder blades. "Holy shit, where have you been? I've been looking all over the place for you. I went to your suite, but no one was there."

Teegan glanced at her watch. A little after seven. Damn, she'd hoped to have at least another hour of solitude before anyone came looking for her. "What's going on?"

"Did you hear about Juliet?"

"What? That she and Wes were making out?"

"No. She ca—" Jessica snapped upright in her seat. "Wait, what? Why were Wes and Juliet making out? When?"

Teegan shooed the comment away with a sway of her hand, too exhausted to put effort into a real response. "Last night."

Jess's shoulders tensed. "Is that why Juliet called off the wedding?"

It was Teegan's turn to jolt upright, almost sloshing her OJ and champagne all over the table. "What did you say?"

"Juliet called off the wedding. Canceled everything. The DJ. The food. All of it. The wedding isn't happening."

Motherfu—

Of course it wasn't.

I plan on telling Juliet my secret the night before her wedding. So you probably don't want to be around for that.

That's what he'd told Teegan when they first made their arrangement. She hadn't given it much thought when he'd told her, but now it made perfect sense. If he told Juliet he was back in the NFL after she was married, she'd be stuck. But if he said something to her before her vows, then there would be a chance they could reconcile. She could call the whole thing off and be with him. And Teegan wouldn't be around to distract either one of them.

Asshole. He'd played Teegan. Gotten her to bring him along so that he could get a one-on-one audience with his ex. Man, what an idiot Teegan had been. She fell right into it. She really was desperate. Oh, how Juliet and Wes must be laughing at her right now.

"Holy shit," Teegan said, her hand clutching the glass hard enough to shatter it.

"I know. That's what I said."

"No," Teegan said, flicking her gaze to Jessica. "Holy shit— Juliet and Wes are back together."

"How can he—? How can they—? He's with you."

"Oh my God!" came another shout, and then rushed footsteps across the concrete patio.

Saylor and Avery were also breathing heavily as they dropped into the remaining two chairs at the table. Both women looked as equally put together as Jess in coordinating yoga outfits, oversized designer sunglasses, and ponytails. Teegan felt severely lacking in her worn T-shirt and shorts, and hair in a messy gather on top of her head. The black bags she probably had under her eyes from lack of sleep probably didn't help either.

"Did you hear what happened?" Avery asked.

"Wes and Juliet are back together," Jess said.

"*What?*" Avery and Saylor said in unison.

"But he's with you," Saylor said with enough indignation in her tone to make Teegan's chest lighten a little. At least a few people had her back.

"He's not." Teegan downed the rest of her glass in one shot. When finished, she held it in the air, signaling the waiter to bring another. She held up four fingers.

Four? he mouthed.

She nodded. Yep.

Jess propped her elbow onto the table and dropped her chin onto her fist. "What do you mean you and Wes aren't together?"

Teegan sighed. Here it goes. "Wes and I were never together. It was an arrangement so we both could get through this shit show of a wedding."

"But, I thought—"

"Then why were you—"

"*What?*"

All three women said over one another.

The waiter brought a tray of mimosas, resting each one in the center of the table. The other ladies attempted to slide one her way, but Teegan blocked them, hoarding all four glasses on her side. Jess glanced up at the waiter, who seemed to read her mind about something because he nodded and scurried away.

Teegan plucked a drink from the table and drank a long swallow, giving her a few seconds to get her thoughts together. "I couldn't bear to come to Mexico alone. It was the last Delta Gam wedding, and I refused to be dateless. Again. Wes wanted to attend the wedding so he could—I thought—get back at Juliet, but apparently, it was so he could get back together with her."

"But, you two are together," Saylor said, her Southern voice full of pity. "You said you were in love."

"All a concoction so you girls wouldn't feel sorry for me. And it worked. Everyone believed us."

"Of course we did!" Avery said. "You were happy!"

"Maybe for a short while. But it wasn't real. And I fell for it just as much as you all did. He doesn't love me. He still loves Juliet."

"I don't believe that," Saylor said. "I watched you two together. You care about one another."

"Me too," Jess said. "I was envious of the connection you two have. It's real."

First drink done, Teegan moved onto the second. "Wes apparently missed the memo then. They were making out like horny teenagers at the ice machine last night."

Gasps exploded from across the table.

She let out a harsh laugh. "But not before he and I got it on."

"Oh, honey." Avery rubbed her arm.

"Wait," Jessica said. "You had sex? Real sex? Even though you weren't truly together?"

Teegan eyed her. "That's what you're choosing to focus on right now?"

"Yes," Jessica said. "Because that means something. How was it?"

Groaning, Teegan said, "So freaking good. Amazing, even."

"See!" Jessica said. "Men don't have half-assed sex with women they don't care about. If he wanted to make it good for you, then he cares."

"About his own satisfaction," Teegan grumbled.

"Where is he now?" Avery asked.

Teegan tipped her head back and drank some more, feeling the initial haze of a buzz starting to finally take hold. "No clue. I walked out last night and haven't been back to the room. He's probably shacked up in Juliet's suite by now."

"So what are you going to do?" Saylor asked as the waiter brought three filled mimosas.

Teegan took the glasses and handed them to her friends. "Guess I go back home to the pathetic, single-girl life I had before."

Jessica smacked her on the shoulder.

"Ow." Teegan rubbed the spot.

"Stop saying that," Jessica said. "You're not pathetic. You have friends, we love you, and you're going to get through this. You're going to meet a guy who makes you even happier, and you're going to get married, and be happily miserable like the rest of us."

"But I don't want anyone else," she said. "I want Wes." She blew a breath. "Wanted. Past tense. Before he was a douche banana, making me think he and I could actually love each other for real."

"This sucks," Avery said.

"It does," Saylor said.

"What did you say?" another voice said.

All heads spun toward where it came from.

Misty. Shit. Perfect ending to an already effed-up weekend.

"Did you just say that you wanted my brother? And why did you call him a douche banana?" Her face wasn't angry per se but wasn't exactly pleasant either.

Unease settled over the table, each woman taking turns looking in a different direction like they weren't paying attention to Misty's growing ire.

"Everything's fine," Teegan said. "Don't worry. It all ended as it should have."

Misty slid a dark chair to the table, the nasty screeching noise of metal against concrete grating on Teegan's already pounding head. She stopped next to Teegan, sat, and looked at her. "Speak. Now."

Teegan's shoulders slumped as her stomach turned over. "Your brother and I told people we were in love."

"I know. What else?"

"We slept together."

Misty's nostrils flared. "Go on."

"Then he made out with Juliet."

Jessica jumped in. "And now he and Juliet are back together. Juliet canceled the wedding and everything."

Misty's face showed confusion. "No, they're not."

"They are," Avery said. "Teegan said she saw them kissing last night. And now the wedding is off."

"And?" Misty asked. "How did you come to the conclusion that Juliet and Wes are together?"

The women looked at Misty like she had lost her marbles.

"Uh, it's called deductive reasoning," Jess said.

"Really?" Misty said with a snap. "Then what do you call hearing it straight from the source?"

Eight eyes blinked around the table, silence ticking away.

"I talked to Wes," she went on. "He came by last night. Really bad timing. So we chatted a bit more today. He doesn't want Juliet any more than Juliet wants him."

"I don't understand," Teegan said, massaging the pain at her temples. "They were kissing."

"They both agreed it was a mistake. Juliet told him it made her realize that if she was trying to kiss another man, she must not love LJ the way she should. And it wouldn't be fair to marry him just because of what he can give her."

"That means...they're not together?" Teegan could barely get the words out. The realization hit her hard that Wes didn't want Juliet and he hadn't lied to Teegan about bringing him to the wedding. Was there still a chance he wanted Teegan? Had their weekend together meant as much to him as it did to her?

No, it didn't. He'd told her as much.

"Definitely not together," Misty said, snatching one of Teegan's mimosas. She sipped, then said, "What does that mean to you?"

"I—I thought—When Jess said—and I saw them kissing—" Teegan didn't know what she was thinking right now. It was so much to process. It was also too much to hope. If he didn't want Juliet, could Teegan and Wes have a chance to be happy together? Before the thought got her too excited, another thought processed. The primary reason Teegan had never pursued Wes in the first place. "What about you?"

Misty's auburn eyebrows lowered. "Me?"

"Yes," Teegan went on. "How would you feel about your best friend dating your brother?"

Misty's smile was quick and efficient in smashing any lingering worry Teegan felt. "If you two are going to put real effort into this thing, then I say do it. But it needs to be all the way, none of this lying bullshit anymore."

Teegan's chest filled with hope. "You'd seriously be okay with it?"

Her best friend's hazel eyes glimmered with adoration. "I'd be more than okay with it."

But...Teegan's optimism faded immediately as she recalled her conversation with Wes last night. "He doesn't want me like that. He told me he needs to focus on football. A relationship would complicate his comeback."

"Say what?" all the girls said.

"Comeback?"

"What comeback?"

"He's playing football again?"

"Give it a rest for a second, will ya, ladies?" Misty chided. She turned to Teegan. "He was scared. Terrified even."

Terrified? Of what? Teegan?

What did that mean? Did he want her? It's what she wanted but hearing that it could be a real possibility made her heart race. Talk about terrifying. She was scared shitless. This was Wes. The man she'd wanted for so long. The man she'd never considered as a remote possibility. Now, based on what Misty was saying...

Misty picked something out of her teeth and went on. "Wes has always been the weaker of the two of us. Even when we were little. I can remember the time when he was ten years old, and he swore there was a monster in his closet. I kept telling him monsters didn't exist, but he wouldn't let it go until I went and checked. There I was, his kid sister, flashlight in hand, shining it into his dark closet."

"What happened?" Saylor asked. "Did he feel better after that?"

"Hell no," Misty said. "He pissed his pants, and it dripped all over the floor into a huge puddle. It was disgusting."

"That's not how the damn story went, and you know it," a deep, masculine voice said behind her.

Misty laughed, loud and obnoxious. "I know. But my version is so much better."

Teegan's entire body went into awareness mode. Her nerve endings sizzled to attention. Her skin felt too tight. The cotton of her clothes too rough.

She didn't look at him. Not yet.

"Ladies," Wes said. "Do you mind if I have a moment with Teegan?"

"Sure."

"Yes."

"Of course. Take all the time you need."

Jessica, Saylor, and Avery got to their feet, grinning like they'd just had an atomic orgasm that was still going.

"We'll be right over here if you need us." The women drifted in the direction of the resort, but nowhere near far enough. They'd still be able to hear every word. Clever.

Misty didn't move.

Wes stood at the edge of the table. Teegan glided her gaze only as high as his waist, her swarming nerves still not allowing her to look all the way up at him.

"Sis? Can you give us a minute?" he asked.

Misty crossed her arms and stared her brother down.

He sighed. "Of course you want to be present for my groveling."

"I want to make sure you don't screw it up, pisser." Misty reclined in her chair with a drink in hand. "Come on. Get on with it."

"No pressure," Wes grumbled. "Thanks."

Teegan still didn't look him in the eye. Wes pulled her chair away from the table so he could kneel in front of her, which pretty much forced their gazes together.

"Hey," he said with a small, hesitant smile.

"Hey," she said back with a tiny flash of hope.

Don't go soft. Guard your heart. He could be letting you down easy.

"What, uh, what happened last night," he started. "What you saw. It wasn't what you think."

The nervousness in his eyes made her hope blossom even more.

"What did I think?" she asked.

"That Juliet and I were kissing."

"You were, weren't you?"

"Well, yeah. But it wasn't kissing-kissing. I didn't enjoy it."

"Is that supposed to make me feel better?"

"Yes. No." He exhaled hard. "I want you to know it didn't mean anything."

"Tell her you're sorry for being an idiot," Misty said.

"I—" His jaw clamped down, and he closed his eyes. When he opened them, he glanced over at his sister. "I'm getting there."

"Get there faster," Misty said. "Stop wasting time."

Wes growled. "I don't know what happened last night. Or why it happened, but I'm glad it did."

"You're glad you kissed Juliet?" She started to stand, deciding she'd heard enough of his pitiful excuse for an apology. But he spoke again.

"I mean that it made me realize I'm done."

"Done?" Teegan and Misty both said.

"No. Not completely done," he said quickly. "Jesus. Why can't I get this right?" He looked at Teegan with a renewed expression. "I mean I'm done with Juliet. With any other woman, for that matter. You're it. I only want you."

The hope in her chest lit into a full-on glow that radiated from head to toe. "You do?"

"I do. While I was kissing Juliet, all I could think about was you. How bad I wanted it to be you. How bad I wanted to return to the suite and pick up where we left off. Minus the arguing, of course."

"Sorry. Now tell her you're sorry," Misty said.

"I'm sorry," he said through tight lips. "For everything. I put you through a lot this weekend, and I'm sorry." He waited, his eyes taking on an anxious glint.

Misty made an impatient sound. "You gonna tell her you love her or what?"

With the slow creep of a smile starting in the corner of his mouth and then spreading, Wes said, "I love you, Teegan. And it's not because my annoying sister is urging me to say it."

A collective girly sigh erupted from where Jess, Avery, and Saylor stood.

"Go on," Misty said to Teegan. "Tell him you love him too."

Smiling back, Teegan gazed into Wes's blue eyes. "I love you too. And it's not because of your sister."

Wes pulled her out of the chair and wrapped her in his arms. Her feet dangled as she put her arms around his neck, her lips immediately searching for his.

They kissed, and it was like it was the first time. They spent a few moments exploring each other, gently caressing until he opened his mouth. The kiss deepened, and his arms tightened. There was nothing in the world that felt as good as Wes holding her and showing her how much he loved her.

"Okay, I think that's enough," Misty said.

They didn't stop.

"Seriously," Misty said. "Kinda gross now."

They pulled apart with a chuckle.

Teegan ran her palm along his stubbled cheek. "You're the only man I've ever wanted."

"You're the only woman I'm ever going to want."

"You mean that?"

"I do," he said, kissing her again.

Misty cleared her throat, and when they didn't pull apart, she repeated the sound louder.

Wes smiled against her lips. "You wanna go somewhere more private?"

"I thought you'd never ask," she said.

Swinging an arm under her, he held her across his broad chest like she weighed nothing.

"We'll see you at the airport," he said as he passed his sister.

"Don't be late!" Misty called out, a smile finally entering her tone.

Teegan gave a quick wave to her friends, who responded with wide, excited smiles of their own.

Epilogue

This was it. The weekend was over. It was supposed to be the end of their time together. Instead, Teegan stood in the suite she'd shared with Wes for the past few days, and they were making plans. Plans for the future.

Teegan could barely contain her excitement.

Picking up her sandals, she slipped them into her suitcase. She went for her makeup bag next. Wes was out on the balcony with a cell phone to his ear, attempting to get his flight from Mexico to Texas swapped for one to New York. He had a few months before football preseason started, and his plan was to come and stay with Teegan for a while. Of course, she'd have to share him with his sister, but Teegan was okay with that. They had to get out of bed at some point to eat and shower anyway, so they might as well visit with other people occasionally.

She was zipping up her brown leather carry-on bag when heavy footsteps came up behind her, then a pair of arms circled her waist. He kissed the back of her neck, making her belly do a little dance. There were major advantages to their difference in height.

"Good news," he said, turning her to face him. "We got the last two first class seats into LaGuardia tonight."

"We don't have to fly in luxury, you know."

"Says the woman with short legs who never has to squeeze anywhere."

Teegan raked a glance down his body, taking in the length. "Good point. You know Misty is going to be pissed, right? We left her and Jim in coach on the flight out here."

He shrugged. "She needs to get her man to buck up some dough then."

Laughing, Teegan put her arms around his midsection and rested her head on his chest. "I love you."

"I love you too." His arms embraced her lower back, and he kissed the top of her head. "It never gets old saying that."

"It doesn't," she agreed. "The first time you said it, I could barely breathe."

"That's because you were under duress, fearing for your life from my psychotic sister."

"That wasn't the first time we said it."

He looked at her in confusion, so she said, "The first time was during the questions game."

His expression warmed at the memory. "That's right. Guess I've always loved you, I just needed time to realize it."

"Oh, good answer, Mr. Romantic." Drawing back, she looked up at him. Gazes connecting, he bent to kiss her. Her body zapped to awareness. Her blood heated, and pulse started to roar. A sound of approval rumbled from deep inside her.

"Again already?" he said. "Damn, woman. I'm gonna have to start intense training to keep up with your insatiable appetite."

"I can't help it. It's you. I can't get enough."

"Good." His hand coasted down her backside to cup her. The blue in his eyes deepened.

He picked her up, wrapping her legs around his waist, and started walking toward to the bed. But a loud knock on the door made him pause.

"Ignore it," she said. "Whoever it is can wait."

Wes deposited her on the bed and started crawling up her body.

Another loud knock. "It's me," Misty's voice called. "You've had plenty of time to get it out of your system, open up."

Wes's eyes slammed closed as his chin hit his chest.

"She has the worst timing," Teegan said.

Releasing a long sigh, Wes pushed off the bed and adjusted his shorts before walking out of the room. Teegan followed at a slow pace, figuring there was no reason to rush.

When he opened the door, Misty and Jim stood on the other side, suitcases at their feet, sunglasses on their heads, and a smile on their faces.

Misty stepped into the room, handing a paper to Wes on her way. "Butler guy told me to give this to you. It's your final bill. I took the liberty to look it over. One hell of a charge for room service last night. What the hell did you guys eat?"

"Why?" Wes asked, his eyes starting to lower to the paper.

Shit! Teegan forgot about the huge tip she'd given Amarosa.

She sprinted forward, trying to snatch the paper out of his hand, but he quickly lifted it up over his head where she couldn't reach.

With a playful tilt to his lips, he said, "Something you want to tell me, Teegan?"

"I, uh...you should know that what's on there was a result of a really big misunderstanding."

"Interesting," he said. "How big?"

"Uh...Massive."

He brought the receipt down to eye level and scanned it, his eyes expanding as he must have located the charge. "Twenty-two hundred dollars?"

"I might've gone a little overboard."

"A little?"

"Okay, a lot. But I was beyond pissed at you. If it helps, think of it as a charitable donation. You made a mother and her son very happy."

His eyebrows rose.

"Great cause. Trust me."

Wes eyed her, his expression suggesting he wasn't nearly as angry as he acted. "This is what I have to look forward to? Any arguments we have will result in you giving away all my money?"

"You're lucky," Misty said from the other side of the room. She'd pulled a beer and a chocolate bar from the mini fridge and was working on ripping the candy open. "If it were me, I wouldn't have spent your money. If I'd have found you with Juliet, you'd be missing a few important body parts."

Misty's husband nodded, grimacing as he sidled up beside her.

Wes winced, looking down at Teegan as she approached. When she reached his side, he put an arm around her and pulled her close. "You're welcome to spend whatever you want."

Misty shrugged, breaking her chocolate in half. She gave one side to Jim and chomped down on her own piece.

"I don't plan on getting mad at you anymore." Teegan looked up at him, meaning it. She was so happy that she might float away right now.

He gave her a sexy smile that had her blood heating as if on reflex. "And I don't plan on doing anything to make you mad."

"Then we shouldn't have a problem. It'll be pure bliss from here on out."

A snort sounded from Misty's corner of the room.

They ignored her because, at the moment, it was pure bliss. They'd have ups and downs; she knew that. But at the moment, everything was perfect.

Wes lowered his head to place his lips on hers—where they belonged, and where she would keep them twenty-three out of twenty-four hours each day. NFL games usually ran for about an hour, after all.

The End!

Excerpt from **IN WALKED TROUBLE**
an Under Covers novel
by Christina Elle

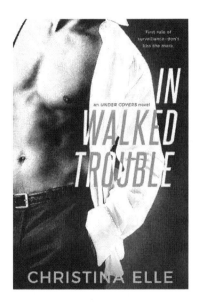

Entangled Publishing, LLC
2614 South Timberline Road
Suite 109
Fort Collins, CO 80525
Visit our website at www.entangledpublishing.com.

Select Suspense is an imprint of Entangled Publishing, LLC.

Edited by Alycia Tornetta
Cover design by Anna Crosswell
Cover art from Deposit Photos

ISBN 978-1-64063-136-6
Manufactured in the United States of America
First Edition July 2017

To the law enforcement officers and their families across our great nation. No one knows how hard this life really is unless you live it. Thank you for putting your lives on the line and for staying tough. I see you.

And to Keith, who willingly gives up valuable time with his family to serve and protect because he sees a greater purpose. The boys and I are proud of you, even if we don't always say it.

IN WALKED TROUBLE

CHAPTER ONE

"I'm not adventurous in bed?" Cassandra Stone said as she gripped the heavy brass handle on the front door of Max's bar and yanked the bastard open. "Well, I'll show him how adventurous I can be."

Cass stepped into the entryway and glanced around. She must have given the door more of a shove than she thought because it slammed against the interior wall, rattling a few picture frames of celebrities. Each famous figure hugged the same bald-headed, wide-smiling man. Sylvester Stallone, Bruce Willis, and...was that Dolly Parton before her third boob job? Hmm, this place wasn't exactly what Cassandra had hoped for.

She was searching for dark and dangerous. Instead, Max's was more glittering lights, sparkles, and Wayne Newton. But whatever, she was on a mission. Plus, it was too damn frigid outside to go looking for another place. This would have to do.

Smoothing stray brown hairs that had pulled loose from her ponytail due to the high winds on Broadway, she hoisted her handbag higher on her shoulder. There had to be someone here who fit what she needed. Dangerous men lurked everywhere, didn't they? More so at bars. But hopefully for her sake, they hung out at places with an illuminated guitar hanging from the ceiling.

Find a man. Go home with him. Do it. And move on.

Simple.

Right?

Right.

The place wasn't crowded or loud. Only a handful of bodies sat along the bar, probably those who snuck in for a drink after a long day of work. A few people sat alone at round tables in the middle of the room. As she scanned the area, inquisitive eyes connected with hers, their expression a mixture of curiosity and a little pity. Or maybe she just perceived it as pity since she felt completely out of her element.

A middle-aged man smirked at her from a table in the far corner. He slouched in his seat, arm draped across the empty chair next to him. He was decent looking. Navy suit, navy tie loosened from his neck, top button of his shirt undone. His hair was more gray than brown and he had deep laugh lines in the corners of his eyes. Just like…

Not going there. Moving on.

A frosty chill crept up from the floor, seeping through her ballet flats and up under the hem of her jeans. It twisted around her legs like a vine growing northward by the second. She instinctively wrapped her arms around herself and rubbed them, trying to create any spark of warmth.

This was ridiculous. If she wanted to find someone, she couldn't stand here all day. She had to find a seat and settle in. Not that Cass had a clue what she was doing, since she'd never picked up anything except produce at the grocery store. But it had to be done.

Put on your big girl panties and lay the sexy down.

Glancing to the back of the room, she spotted two empty seats at the bar. Perfect. One for her and one for her adventurously wild one-night stand.

Cassandra hustled in that direction and hoisted herself onto a barstool. She slapped a hand down on the bar.

"Excuse me, guy back there," she said to the twentysomething bartender. "I need a drink. Whatever's strong and burns like hell on the way down. In fact, make it a double." She was going to need a shit ton more courage for this.

She huffed out a breath and smoothed more errant hairs.

"Rough day, huh?" a deep voice said from her right.

Cass tensed, then spun toward the sound, meeting a set of perfectly white, perfectly straight teeth of a man grinning two seats down. She took in his black dress pants and pressed shirt with sleeves rolled up to his elbows.

Damn, he was good looking. Too clean cut for what she needed though. She sighed. "You have no idea."

It wasn't every day your almost-fiancé decided you weren't exciting enough in bed and told you that he found someone else to fulfill his needs.

Gripping a beer, he twisted to face her. "Wanna talk about it?"

At the full-on glance, an excited thrill skated up her spine. Cropped blond hair, blue eyes, killer smile, dimples.

Everything she *wasn't* looking for.

Very much like Daniel, this man pulled off cocky and confident at the same time. He knew he was God's gift, but also seemed to know he had the goods to back it up. Not that every other man didn't assume he was well equipped to handle women. But this one, with smile broadening, told her he knew *exactly* what to do with his lips, tongue, teeth…and other parts. A shiver ran through her, and then she squashed it, reminding herself what she'd come for.

Dark and dangerous.

Signaling to the chair between them, he asked, "May I?"

She hesitated. "I'm saving it for someone." Technically she was, she just didn't know who yet.

His smile didn't falter. "Really?" His voice was sarcastic, condescending.

"As a matter of fact, yes," she said. "Why did you say it like that?"

Still smiling. "Like what?"

She wished he would take those damn dimples elsewhere.

They were starting to make her forget her mission. He was 100 percent her type and then some. Or at least he was before she started despising hot, sharply dressed men. "Like you just said it."

"How did I just say it?" Deeper dimples, damn him.

"Like you don't believe me." She lifted her chin and glanced away. *Out of sight, out of mind.* "I am. I'm waiting for someone."

The bartender appeared with a shot glass and a large brown bottle. She reached into her purse and pulled out the fifty she'd taken from Daniel's wallet before she walked out. If she was going to get drunk, she was doing it with his money. The bastard.

Cass placed the crisp bill on the bar as the bartender poured the liquor into a short glass, filling it all the way to the top. Perfect. Double, indeed.

"Hmm," the man next to her mused.

She whipped her attention to him. "What was that for?"

"What?"

"That noise you just made."

"What noise?" he asked.

"Stop being coy. That *hmm* noise."

He shifted on the stool and rested an elbow on the bar, seeming to bite back a laugh. "I didn't make a noise."

"Yes, you—" She stopped and cleared her throat. The point was to take the edge off with a drink or two, then go home with a rugged stranger. Not get into a verbal dispute with someone who had the angelic face of a *GQ* model.

"Forget it. I'm waiting for someone, so please finish your beer and move along."

The man propped an elbow on the edge of the bar.

"What's his name?"

"Huh?"

He lifted one eyebrow.

"Oh. Uh." Her cheeks ignited. Not because he'd caught her in a lie. More because it was embarrassing. How could she explain she was looking for a man to have a one-night stand with because her ex-almost-fiancé was an ass? Even worse, because she couldn't satisfy him in the bedroom?

No way.

"It's none of your business," she said and reached for the glass.

"What if I'd like to make it my business?"

Ugh, even his voice was smooth. Like cognac on a cold, winter night, warming her up from the inside out.

Rolling her eyes at her traitorous, needy female body, she said, "You can't. Now please go away."

"Just answer me one question."

She dropped the glass onto the bar top with a thud, spewing large droplets of liquor on the smooth surface, and let out a sigh. Why did he have to be so trying? Yes, she came looking for a one-night stand. Yes, this man was extremely good looking. Yes, he could probably screw her brains thirty ways to Sunday and keep the reverberations going all the way through next Monday. But she wanted dark and dangerous.

She'd done the tall, charming, tax accountant. She wanted a wild, rough, tough, hairy, biker dude.

Someone the complete opposite of Daniel.

"Fine," she said. "One question. Then will you leave me alone?"

His smile grew wider. "Sure."

Yikes. Something that powerful should come with a warning label. Her lady parts gleefully started humming.

Down girls.

After a fortifying breath, Cassandra turned to give the man her undivided attention, and crossed one leg over the opposite knee.

"What's a woman like you doing here?" he asked.

Excuse me? A woman like her?

"What's that supposed to mean? You think I'm not cut out for a bar? Like I'm too conservative?" Daniel had said that, too. That she needed to loosen up. Well, look at her now—at a bar, trying to get laid.

He clasped his hands together, still resting one elbow on the bar. "Not saying that at all. Just seems odd that you're here drinking alone." He gave her a once-over, giving nothing away in his expression. "You're not meeting a man, despite what you said. That's evident from your attire."

Glancing down at her mint green cardigan and jeans, she frowned. She hadn't really thought about changing when she'd stormed out. She'd had an event at school, then came home, found Daniel in bed with *her*, and couldn't process anything except coming here.

Not that she had "bar" attire anyway. She'd been with Daniel for seven years and seriously almost-engaged for the last two. Those bar days were behind her. What did she need a tight top and miniskirt for?

Maybe if you had worn that stuff more regularly, Daniel wouldn't have gone looking elsewhere.

Shut up. That's not true.

So she'd gotten comfortable in her relationship. Who hasn't? She bit back the growing anger and frustration.

"And you sat at the bar," he continued, "rather than a booth, which tells me you're not meeting girlfriends after work. So what is it? Just needed a shot of"—his gaze slid to the drink in front of her and his nose wrinkled—"nuclear waste to end a long work week?"

She threw an unsure glance at the short glass with opaque brown liquid, then came back to him. "Why does it matter to you?"

He lifted one shoulder. "I'm curious."

Cass narrowed her eyes and assessed him. "What did you say

your name was?" He hadn't given it yet and she knew it.

He paused, watching her, too. "Luke."

"Well, Luke, if you must know—"

"Afraid to give me yours?"

She straightened her spine and set her jaw. "Of course not. Why would I be afraid?" She wasn't, but it caught her off guard. She hadn't planned on giving it to anyone tonight.

Names weren't necessary for what she needed.

"How about that name then?"

"*Cassssssandra.*" Damn it, it was out before she could think of something else.

His lips twitched. "Interesting name. How many *s*'s are in that?"

Lips sealed, she stared at him. She should've thought of a bar name. Electra. Tina. Nicolette. Something saucy. She'd have to remember that for Mr. Dangerous.

"Now that we're old friends, *Cassssssandra*, how about we talk about what you're doing here."

The bartender circled back in their direction, saving her from responding. He opened his mouth but saw the full glass still in front of her and stopped. "Still doing okay here?"

She and Luke both nodded.

Cass reached for her glass and lifted it up to her nose, sniffing the content. Yikes. Burn her nose hairs why doesn't it.

"Not sure I would down that if I were you," Luke said, sounding much closer than before.

She turned as he casually maneuvered himself onto the stool directly next to her. "Whoa, buddy. I told you I was saving this seat for someone—"

"And when he shows," he said, settling in. "I'll move. But for now, let's chat."

She caught a quick whiff of something clean and musky.

It took everything she had not to close her eyes and inhale all of it. She crossed her legs again, keeping everything tucked away where it should be.

Scanning the room, she wished her prince of bad-assery would arrive soon and ravage her. She didn't have all night.

The longer she sat here, the quicker her common sense came back. Maybe rushing out wasn't the smartest move. But she'd had to do something. She couldn't sit in that condo for a second longer staring at Daniel and *her*.

He gestured with his chin toward her drink. "That's some pretty strong stuff. You should probably start with something weaker and work up to that."

Realizing she still gripped the shot glass, she sniffed it again and bit back her gag reflex. Oak, wood, more wood, and a hint of burned tree trunk traveled up her nasal passage.

This was going to hurt. But it was necessary if she was going to get through the evening. Dull the pain and all that. Before she could talk herself out of it, she squeezed her eyes shut and threw her head back, downing the shot in one gulp.

Holy hot tamales walking across hot coals in Mexico!

As her head came up, she coughed and choked. Fire raced down her throat, then rocketed back up. Her tongue went numb, her stomach clenched, and she had to catch her breath before flames propelled out and burned the entire place down. That shit was a lot more potent than her usual bahama breeze spritzers.

"Delicious, right?" Luke asked with sardonic lift of his lips.

"Yeah," she croaked. "Love it. Think I'll have another."

She held up a hand for the bartender, who diligently shuffled over.

Before she could make the request—wheezing was all she was good for at the moment—Luke spoke instead.

"She'll have a really big glass of ice water, please. And some peanuts. You guys have those, right?"

The bartender nodded and walked off.

When she finally found the words, she said, "I wanted another drink."

"That's what I got you."

"You know what I mean, a *real* drink. I need it so I can—"

Oookay, maybe she didn't need another round. One more and she'd be flinging every embarrassing secret she had all over this bar.

With interest gleaming in his blue eyes, Luke inched his perfectly chiseled jaw with just the right amount of stubble into her personal space. "So you can what?"

"Nothing. It's none of your business. Are you finished with your beer so you can go?" She had a mission to fulfill and his hot-guy smiles were cramping her style.

Without looking away, he reached into his back pocket, pulled a bill loose from a silver money clip, and held it into the air.

Moments later, the bartender placed a large glass of water, another beer, and a small bowl of peanuts on the bar top.

Luke clicked his bottle on her glass, then nudged the water and nuts in front of her. "Cheers."

She slumped on her stool. "You're not going away anytime soon, are you?"

"Nope. I'm really liking the scenery." Though when he said it, he didn't look around, only at her.

"Don't you have better things to do? Like go gel your impeccable hair?"

His lips lifted behind his glass. "I've got time to kill."

CHAPTER TWO

Luke Calder had come to Max's to blow off some steam. When your days were numbered because a sadistic drug supplier was coming to kill you, you lived up every second you had. With alcohol. He'd needed a distraction to take his mind off his impending fate, and wouldn't you know it—wish granted.

Luke had watched Cassandra storm into the place and scan the area, and then she'd hesitated on what to do next. It was brief, but it was there. He guaranteed no one else picked up on it, but they didn't have his skills in observation. Her pause had been enough to put a ding in his armor. That one vulnerable second had caught him. She could say all the bull she wanted about meeting someone. If there was anyone, he wasn't coming.

"So back to the topic at hand," he said. "Why are you here, Cassandra?"

"I could ask you the same thing, Luke." She jutted her chin out. The move was quickly growing on him. "Why are *you* here? Hard day at the office crunching numbers? Wanted to blow off some steam?"

Testy, testy. Why the dislike for a white-collar man? "Yeah, something like that."

"So, you're what?" She took in his dress shirt and suit pants, and the corner of her lips tightened. "Accountant? Financial advisor? Stockbroker?"

Again, he sipped his beer, then nodded.

He and his DEA team leader, Ash Cooper, had just gotten back from a court hearing in DC. Luke liked to dress up more than his teammates anyway, but today he was more formal than usual. He could see why she'd assume his job matched his current attire.

A tiny, deep groove formed between her eyebrows. "Well, which one?"

"Teacher," he said, fighting like hell to keep a straight face.

"Teacher?" She barked a laugh. "You, sir, are no teacher. I work with teachers. You're dressed much too nice to—"

Cassandra froze, realizing what she'd done, and a wide smile swept across his face. *Gotcha.*

Her face turned red. "Damn you. You did that on purpose, didn't you? How? How did you know?"

"Know what?" he asked in his best unassuming voice.

The groove between her eyebrows got deeper and she grunted. "Stop doing that. You know what I mean."

"Do I?" He was a guy and therefore an immature ass at times. He found entertainment where he could, and this brunette firecracker was certainly fascinating.

Her eyes widened and her lips curled inward. Before the vein on her forehead popped, he said, "All right, all right. I made an educated guess. Also…" He reached toward her left hip.

She froze. "What are you—?"

"Because of this." He pulled a card attached to a zip cord on her waistband. Her school ID that she'd obviously forgotten to take off.

He kept the cord pulled tight so he could read the information listed.

Cassandra Stone

School Guidance Counselor

John C. Carver High School

With a tug, she pulled the card out of his grip. "How dare you. That's personal information. I don't know anything about you and now you know my full name, where I work, and what I do." She pushed the empty shot glass away and dropped her forehead onto the bar with a *thunk*. "Oh, no. This is bad. This is really bad. What was I thinking? I can't do this. How can I do this? I can't. That's how. Oh. My. God."

He'd had enough experience with women to know now was not the right time to laugh, comment, or make a suggestion, so he swallowed it down and tried to talk her off the ledge.

"Hey," he said, "You okay?" When she didn't lift her head, he said, "Cassandra, look at me."

She shook her head and a few loose strands of hair floated freely.

"Cassandra, come on. It's not that big of a deal. You can trust me."

That did it. She surged upright and turned to him. "Trust you? *Trust* you? Ha! I don't even know you. I've spent the better— well, actually the worst—part of the last seven years with my ex-almost-fiancé, who looks just like you by the way, only to find out that he was a lying, no good cheat who was banging his coworker because she was more outgoing in the bedroom. Do you know what that's like?"

Okay, now we're getting somewhere.

Cassandra Stone. School Counselor. Her ex was too

much of a douche to propose, but liked it hard core, and an even bigger douchebag because he'd made her feel bad about it. But wait… "Ex- *almost*-fiancé?"

"Yes," she said straight-faced.

"How can you—?"

Her eyes narrowed and he could have sworn she was about to summon the power of Thor and shoot lightning bolts right out of them.

His hands went up in surrender. "So you and your…almost-

fiancé got into a fight," he guessed. "And now you're here to..."
Hell, he had no idea. He knew what women liked in the bedroom,
not in a relationship. He was usually long gone by the time the
women he'd slept with acted like this. "Help me out here, Cassandra. Did you guys get into a fight?"

She nodded.

"Okay," he said. "What was it over? The other woman?"

She slanted her head to the side and stared him down.

"Are you a tax accountant?"

"No."

"Stockbroker. You gotta be a stockbroker."

Shaking his head, he said, "Try again."

"Some sort of Christian Grey type. Lots of money and power,
right?"

He smirked. "Yeah." He did like money and power.

Her eyes lit up. "Yes?"

"Sure, we'll go with that." He didn't usually get into specif-
ics of his real job when he met women. Their time together was
always short-lived, so it didn't matter much.

Plus, he liked the idea of being whoever the woman fantasized
about. In this case, Cassandra was so hell-bent on pegging him as
some stodgy money guy that he wasn't going to burst her bubble.

Her shoulders dropped as she picked up her water, swirling the
straw inside the glass. "You're just like Daniel. I want someone
different. Someone dangerous. Someone who appreciates the way
I like to have sex. And I *do* like to have sex. Don't you doubt that."

He was in the process of placing his drink to his lips, but her
comment made him choke on his own saliva. He lowered the beer,
coughing. Then, of course, because she'd said sex, he started to
imagine what she'd be like in bed. What she'd feel like beneath
him. The image he conjured of her brunette hair spread across his
pillow, looking up at him with those green eyes immediately ignited a flush of heat over him.

Clearing his throat, he said, "No doubting here." None what-soever.

There was plenty about her that he wanted. Her full lips, her bright green eyes, and that trim physique. Oh, and her smart-mouth. He loved a woman with a smart-mouth. They usually told you exactly what and where they wanted it in the bedroom. And he was *real* good at following directions.

"He said I was vanilla." She lounged an elbow on the bar. "Vanilla. Can you believe that? Me." Her gaze met his and held. There was a lot of hurt and regret buried deep, but there was determination, too. Good. Her ex hadn't fully broken her down. No woman deserved to feel unworthy. Especially not in the bedroom.

"I don't want to be vanilla," she went on. "I want to be chocolate. Or even swirl. Or freaking Chunky Monkey. I could totally be Chunky Monkey, don't you think?"

The way her expression opened wider with hope made him want to tell her anything she wanted to hear. He was good at that—pleasing women. But this time he actually wanted to mean it.

"I think you can be anything you want to be," he said.

Her face brightened. "Yeah?"

"Yep."

"You're sweet." She sucked some water through her straw, then said, "Still doesn't mean we're sleeping together."

"It doesn't?" Had he asked? He was pretty sure he hadn't yet. That was usually something he would remember.

"Nope."

"Why would you think we're going to sleep together?"

"We're not," she said. "I can't."

"You can't," he repeated. But didn't she just say she wanted to be some sort of crazy food? Luke had tried just about everything in bed, so he'd be up for whatever she had in mind. Hell, he was always up for a woman showing him something new. Chunky Monkey sounded painful, but maybe it was the good kind of pain.

"Nope. You're not right. You're…" she said, gesturing to him, "clean-cut, chiseled, sexy."

He blinked a few times. "That's a problem?" It had never been a problem before. Like, ever.

"Tonight, it is." She latched onto the straw again, taking another long pull of water. "I don't do guys like you anymore. I'm into hard-core, tattoo-covered, foul-mouthed bikers."

He nearly choked again on his beer. He should just put the thing down and stop trying. Letting his eyes do a wide scan of the room, he only spotted regular, everyday people.

Guys in suits. Ladies in casual tops and slacks. A family of four at a booth in the corner by the door. No hard-core bikers in sight.

"So that's who you're waiting for?"

She nodded.

"Do you…know any hard-core, dangerous bikers?"

"Nope. That's why I'm here. I'm sure one'll be along shortly."

Again, he glanced around the bar. When his attention came back to her, he didn't see any change in her expression to indicate that her plan might be flawed. Instead, there was nothing but the intense haze of the alcohol buzz taking over her brain.

"Okay, let me get this straight," he started. "You came here tonight because you and your ex-almost-fiancé, who is a tax accountant, not a biker, had a fight over his sexual needs, so you stormed out still wearing your work clothes and school ID in order to find someone else who is a biker, so you could…do what exactly?" He was starting to get the gist, but he wanted to hear her say it.

After another long suck on the straw, then the nasty gurgling sound at the bottom of the cup because it was empty, she said, "To sleep with him. Don't you see? I'm vanilla. I need to prove that I've got Cinnamon Buns or Cherry Garcia in me."

Who? And what?

"*Okay*," he said, drawing the syllables out. "But it has to be a biker."

"Yes. Well, no. But he has to be big, mean, and dangerous. I can handle it. I'm ready to rock his world. I can be adventurous in bed."

Luke bit down on his lower lip to keep his smile in check. "I'm sure you can." He believed her. The woman had a lot of fight in her. Besides, it was always the conservative ones who torched the bed sheets.

"So, you see," she went on, "that's why I need you to leave. I need this seat open for when he shows up." She glanced at her watch. "And *Outlander* comes on at nine. I'm kinda pressed for time, so it would be great if you could get a move on."

He wasn't going anywhere.

"How dangerous does this guy need to be?"

She lowered her chin so she could look at him directly and deepened her voice. "Very."

"Does he have to own a bike?"

She looked up at the ceiling, thinking. "I guess not.

Leather would be nice though."

Leather. Really?

"Well, I guess not the leather. But definitely big, mean, and hairy."

It took all he had not to snort.

"This is a lot harder than I thought it'd be," she said with her bottom lip popped. "I figured it would be like the movies—a girl goes to a bar and then she's swarmed with men wanting to take her home. This is nothing like that."

Spearing him with her direct gaze, she said, "Where are all the hot, eligible men who want to have sex with me?"

Navy Suit at the table a few feet away perked up and turned her way. He fixed his loosened tie and wagged his eyebrows in her direction. Grinning, he started to stand, but Luke shot him a *don't even think about it* glare. Navy Suit dropped the smile and slinked back down into his chair.

Not only was she acting out of hurt and embarrassment because of her ex, but now she had the liquor in her system to compete with, too. Luke wasn't letting any of the a-holes in this place take advantage of her.

Luke turned to Cassandra, who seemed to have wilted in her own seat. "There are plenty of men who would go home with you tonight."

Leaning over the bar, still propping her chin on her fist, she said, "Meh." Then she yawned and blinked her watery eyes. "Sure wish they'd come forward soon then. It's getting late."

He snuck a peek at his Rolex. Seven fifteen. Real late. Party animal, this one.

Luke waved an arm in the air, signaling for the bartender. Once he appeared in front of them, Luke gestured with a tilt of his head toward Cassandra. "Do you have the number for a taxi company?"

Cassandra sat up straighter. "Wait, what?" Through another huge, open-mouthed yawn, she said, "I don't need a taxi. I'm good." Then she fell forward, dropping her forehead on the smooth mahogany bar.

Good. Right.

After about a minute of no movement, Luke tapped

Cassandra on the shoulder. "Hey, wake up."

She mumbled something incoherent and flicked a hand out to shoo him away.

"No, seriously," he said, poking her again. "Are you sleeping?"

"Yes."

Laughter bubbled up from his chest. "Your taxi will be here soon. We should get you up and moving so you don't miss it."

"You go ahead," she said, face still buried. "I'm just gonna wallow in my defeat here with all the men who don't want to have sex with me tonight."

"What will it take? A viable offer?"

Still hunched over, her body tensed and she craned her neck to look at him. "A what?"

"A viable offer," he repeated. "Is that what you need? So tonight doesn't feel like it was in vain?"

Her expression was blank, but it seemed like a few wheels were spinning. Very slowly, because the hamster was drunk, but spinning nonetheless.

He zeroed in on her lips, which he noticed were pink, plush, and totally kissable. An image of the two of them back at her place filled his vision. He liked what his mind conjured up. They'd do it once when he carried her into the entryway, again on the kitchen counter, and a third time in her bedroom for good measure.

"I want to sleep with you." It almost surprised him how quickly the desire hit him. Not because she wasn't desirable. More because of how fast the feeling came since their very unorthodox conversation.

She blinked, then sat up straight. "You don't count. I can't sleep with you, because you're—"

"Nothing like your ex, I assure you."

She closed one eye and assessed him through the other. "How?"

He loved women. All women. But only one at a time, and battle lines were very clearly marked while they were together. No womanizing or cheating. Just a good time and phenomenal sex.

"Men love sex," he conceded. "So I won't deny that Daniel and I have that very much in common. But I enjoy it with only one woman at a time, and I never engage in anything that isn't open and honest." Her posture loosened a little, so he continued, "All men have unique sexual needs, but so do women. And it's a man's responsibility to see to it the woman he's with is taken care of. Her needs come first. She should be sated and exhausted every single time. If she's not..." He let out a quick chuckle. "Well, he's not doing his job then, is he?"

Her expression suggested he'd said he was a small furry animal and she wanted to pet him. Wide, open eyes stared back. Mouth slightly open. Head tilted so far that it almost rested on one shoulder. "Would you like to have sex tonight?"

"Uh," he said, taken aback.

"I should tell you in an effort of full disclosure," she went on, "that I didn't shave because I ran out of the house so fast. But you can look past that, right? I mean, it's free sex. Men don't turn that down, do they?"

There were *so* many things he could respond with after such a huge opening. He was definitely interested and he'd be more than happy to show her just how much. But she didn't need a horndog right now. Or a one-night stand. What she needed was someone to help her home so she could sleep off her condition and regroup about her relationship in the morning.

Being the good guy really sucked. Or didn't suck, as it were. Because if she sucked—

Never mind.

"Hey." The bartender appeared in front of them and pointed toward the exit. "Your ride's here."

She snapped out of whatever thoughts she was processing. "Oh, yeah. Thanks." Then she turned to Luke. "Is that a yes?" Her expression was so hopeful that he almost picked her up and carried her out of there. She deserved to feel wanted. No woman should ever doubt her worth in a relationship. And no man should ever give her need to question it. Screw her ex-almost-whatever for making her second-guess herself.

"It's a *not tonight*," he replied.

Her lips flattened into a thin line. "Of course it is. I'm like a pariah. Can't even get a guy I don't know to sleep with me." Stretching her arms out wide, she raised her voice. "I'm sex repellent. Nobody wants what I have going on in my pants." Letting out another big yawn, she reached for her purse hanging on the back of her chair and draped it over her shoulder. "Whatever. Jamie Fraser's waiting for me at home. He never disappoints. Even likes his women hairy as a beast. Eighteenth century au naturel is where it's at." She might've tried to wink, but it was more of squeezing both eyes closed and wrinkling her nose.

Time to go. She was turning into a drunk lunatic.

He held his jacket open so she could slip her arms in.

Wrapping it around herself, she closed the front and inhaled deeply. "Thank you."

"For what?" he asked as he unfolded his cuffs to cover his forearms.

Cassandra gave him a sweet, crooked smile and patted his chest. "Offering your jacket. Listening. Not judging."

There was something about her warm hand on his chest that did funny things to his insides. The small, seemingly insignificant gesture of thanking him made his throat constrict.

Their gazes met and held.

Okay, she was a cute, drunk lunatic.

Luke followed Cassandra's unsteady steps toward the door and out into the freezing night. More than a few times he reached out to steady her balance and worried if she'd even make it to her place in the condition she was in.

He opened the back door of the idling taxi for her.

"Thanks again." Another yawn as she swayed in place.

"You gonna be okay to get home?"

Her gaze flitted around not really focusing on one particular thing. "I'm going home?"

He rolled his eyes and grinned. "Get in." Sliding in beside her, he closed the door. She wasn't his responsibility, but he sure as hell wasn't going to leave the woman in the backseat of a cab in Baltimore.

"Where to?" the driver asked.

Luke looked to Cassandra, who had already cozied up onto the opposite side of the backseat. She held his jacket closed tightly around her neck, rested her head on the window, and breathed deeply with eyes closed.

Shaking his head, Luke responded, "Nineteenth Street."

She could come back with him and sleep it off. Then he'd take her wherever she needed in the morning.

CHAPTER THREE

Cass stretched her arm over her head, breathing in the morning. She hadn't slept that well in a long time. Once her head had hit the pillow, she was O-U-T. It felt great to get so much uninterrupted sleep.

What a crazy night she'd had. Walking in on Daniel and *her*, in the bed he shared with Cass had hurt, which made her irrational, she realized now. Good thing she'd talked some sense into herself and decided not to—

Cass took in the sight of the small bedroom. White walls.

Navy comforter. Navy curtains. Dark wood dresser in front of her.

None of which were hers.

Where in the hell was she?

Luke.

She blew out a breath. Damn it, she hadn't talked crap into herself. He'd been the one who'd helped her. Talked with her. Offered his jacket. Called her a taxi. Luke had said a woman's needs came first and that he was always open and honest with women he slept with. One at a time, he'd said.

Good to know some of those men still existed.

But how embarrassing. She'd spewed all her craptastic relationship drama all over him last night. Ugh. Why had she even listened to herself when she'd said she needed to get revenge on Daniel by having a one-night stand? What would it have proved? Not a thing. Only that she could stick something long and hard where she needed it for one night. Big whoop.

Cass sat up and threw her legs over the side of the bed. What's done was done. Time to get a move on. She needed to get in touch with Daniel and not-so-politely explain that he could shack up with his new bedmate from now on because Cass wasn't giving up their newly decorated condo.

She wore the same clothes from the night before. Luke's suit jacket draped across the end of the bed. Her purse rested on the dresser, so she reached for it. Head pounding, she pulled her cell out of her bag.

8:23 a.m.

She also had a reminder notice on her screen.

10 a.m.: Miguel at Patterson Park with Ronan. Stop him!

Her body jolted to attention. She needed to go! She needed to stop her student from ruining his life.

Swiping a finger across her phone's screen, she searched for her Uber app to request a ride. She checked her location on the interactive map—19th Street, which was more than twenty minutes away from Patterson Park—and scanned for a driver nearby. She needed to get home, grab her winter clothes, and get over to the park ASAP. With any luck, a car could be sitting outside in five.

She selected a driver who was a few minutes away and quickly gathered up her purse, throwing her phone inside.

Cassandra opened the bedroom door to find the living room empty. She ventured to the stairs to seek Luke out, thank him for his help last night, and then be on her way.

Footsteps and clanging sounded overhead in the kitchen.

She placed a foot on the first step, then heard female voices and stilled. Gripping the railing for balance, Cass tuned in.

"Over my dead body," a female voice shouted. "*I'm* going to squeeze them!"

"Screw you," another woman said just as loud. "You don't do it right. You're always too rough."

"Ha! You wish you had my firm grip," the first voice said.

"Luke likes the way I do it."

"On days I'm not around, maybe."

Firm grip? Luke likes it?

"What can I do for him?" a third, mousy voice asked.

What the—? Cass tiptoed to the top step and placed her ear to the door.

"Well, when he gets out of the shower," the second voice continued, "he's gonna be ravenous. Who's gonna oblige him?"

"I will," the first said. "It's my turn. You two gave it to him yesterday morning."

WTF. This was getting out of hand. What happened to one woman at a time? Honesty? And a woman's needs first?

All a load of bull.

Just like Daniel.

Motherfu—

"I'm not playin'," the second voice said. "You squeeze 'em, and I'll see to it you never squeeze nothin' again."

If she had to listen to these women get Luke off on the other side of the door, she might be sick. Maybe while they were busy arguing over who was going to service Luke, Cass could sneak out the front door and catch her Uber.

Another pair of heavy footsteps sounded and the women hushed one another.

"Ladies, ladies," Luke said through a laugh. "There's plenty of me to go around."

Cass's hands curled into fists. What a dill weed. He was all sweet last night talking that shit about honesty and fidelity. Right. And here he was with a gaggle of women at home meeting *his* every need.

"What about the girl downstairs?" the mousy voice asked. "Shouldn't we wait for her?"

"Nah," Luke said. "Let's go ahead and get started. When she wakes up she can join in."

Think again, buddy.

Footsteps continued and then she heard what sounded like three sets of kissing sounds. Then female giggles.

Oh. My. God. Change in plans. Bum rush the door, knock out anyone in her way, and forty-yard dash it out the front. She'd be damned if she turned into a Stepford in his brothel. He'd already thrown her in the basement for crying out loud.

But before she could, the pressure against her ear evaporated. Gravity shifted and she found herself falling forward toward a brown checkerboard linoleum floor. Her hands shot out, preparing for impact, but they were about three seconds too late. Her cheek and shoulder hit, sending a slice of white-hot pain down the entire left side of her body. She sucked in a breath and gritted her teeth. That hurt like a bugger.

Worse, when she tilted her head up, a pair of polished black boots stood in front of her.

"You're awake," Luke said in a humorous tone.

His open palm appeared in her view, but she slapped it away. Rude, yes. But her pride hurt pretty deep right now.

Pushing aside the embarrassment, she got to her feet and brushed her hands down the front of her jeans. "Yes. I'm awake. And I'll be going now."

Cass stepped forward, but Luke moved in front of her like an impenetrable brick wall. He wasn't a big man. More lean in stature than bulky. He was in a fitted long-sleeved shirt and cargo pants, looking just as put together and confident as if he wore a suit and tie. A quality she found very appealing.

Another reason why she needed to be on her way.

Slowly lifting her chin to meet his gaze, she clenched her jaw. "Out of my way, please."

His cool blue eyes watched her, making her squirm. "Why the rush?"

"No rush," she lied, trying to step around him. "I just have to be going." Far, far away from Hugh Hefner and his team of ball squeezers.

He maneuvered to block her way and crossed his arms. "Join me in the dining room first, then I can take you where you need to go. I'm heading out—"

"No thanks. I can take myself."

His eyebrows crunched and his lip puckered in something resembling annoyance and confusion.

Good, her feelings exactly.

"Fine," he said. "I won't take you anywhere." He hitched a thumb over his shoulder and twisted toward the dining room. "But the ladies—"

A half-hysterical laugh bursted out, cutting him off. "Oh, I heard *everything* the ladies said. No thanks. I've had my fill of men and their extra women, remember?"

"What are you talking about?" He twisted again toward the dining room. "They—"

"Like to service you and squeeze your balls. I heard all about it." She sidestepped him and shuffled through the kitchen toward the open doorway. Over her shoulder, she called, "Not my kind of thing, so I'll be going now. Nice knowing you. Thanks for your help last night."

She made it through the doorway and came to a skidding halt. Three women with wide, wrinkled eyes stared back, mouths open.

They sat at a table covered in food. Scrambled eggs, bacon, coffee, muffins, bagels, and a pitcher of freshly squeezed orange juice.

One who looked to be in her late sixties with bottle-brown hair, a round midsection, and low-cut sweater cracked a smile first. Actually it was more of a smirk. "I'm up for squeezin' balls just as much as the next gal. But if I'm doin' it, it ain't Luke's I'm squeezin'.'"

Another woman, much more petite than the first, wearing a pink sweater and pearls looked away. "Oh, Estelle."

The third, white-haired and heavyset, shook her head. "I agree. We all heard the poor girl. You didn't have to repeat it."

Estelle shrugged and reached for the spoon in the large bowl of scrambled eggs. She scooped the food and flopped a pile onto her plate. "Just settin' the record straight, Maybel. I

love me some balls, but I prefer ones that are a little more… ripe." She looked over Cass's shoulder presumably at Luke standing behind her. "No offense, Lukie. You're a doll. But I enjoy my men like my steak. Well-seasoned and leathery."

Luke rested a hand on Cass's back and pointed with the other. "Cassandra, please meet Estelle, Maybel, and Celia."

God. Had she really said *balls* in front of elderly women?

"I…I… I'm sorry." She could have cooked an additional

serving of eggs on her face for as hot as it burned. "I had no idea…I thought…" She looked over her shoulder at Luke, who was grinning, then back to the women at the table. "I heard you say…"

"Forget it." Luke pressed against her spine, nudging her toward an empty seat, and urged her down to sit. Picking up the white china plate in front of her, he started placing food on it.

"Don't forget the OJ." Estelle's lips twitched. "Freshly squeezed with Maybel's firm grip."

Celia, the one wearing pearls, appeared to be choking on something.

Luke sat at the head of the table, his front to the sliding glass door that filtered bright winter light in. He filled his own plate and then began to eat.

Cass glanced at her plate. Back at Luke. At the older women. The kitchen table. The front door. Back at the basement door.

What. The. Hell. Was. Going. On. Here?

"Are you feeling all right, dear?" Maybel asked.

"Yes, fine," she said.

"Your face is a very deep shade of red," Maybel continued. "Are you hot? I meant to turn the heat down.

With the frigid temperatures outside, the damn furnace runs constantly. Be glad you and Luke were in the basement.

Much cooler down there. My bedroom upstairs is a sauna." To prove her point, she pinched her sleeveless cotton shirt at the chest and pulled it away from her body.

"I'm fine. Thank you," Cass said.

Wait a minute… Her bedroom upstairs? Jesus, they all *lived* together! Not to mention that none of them seemed at all fazed by Cass's presence. Was it customary for Luke to bring random women from bars to his grandmother's house?

It was her turn to cough and choke.

In one quick motion, Luke jumped from his seat and pulled her out of her chair, spinning her around. Her vision whirled, so she laid a hand on his solid chest to get her bearing before focusing on his worried gaze.

"You okay?" he asked.

She nodded, afraid to say anything for fear the coughing would start all over.

Her phone made a chirping sound and buzzed in her purse, making her brain clear up immediately.

Her Uber! She leaped away from him. "I have to go."

"Wait, what?" Luke said. "Where? Stay and I'll—"

She started out of the room and spoke over her shoulder. "Can't. I have an appointment. Thanks so much for your help last night." She froze and looked at the older women. "He, uh, didn't *help me*, help me last night. He just gave me a ride here because I drank too much. Nothing, you know, like *that* happened…here. In this house. With all of you here." How embarrassing would this moment have been if she'd actually slept with Luke? She didn't want to think about it.

The women blinked, but didn't comment.

Right. *Shut it, Stone, and get going.* "Thanks again. And... good-bye."

"But—" Luke started.

She was already out the front door and jogging down the steps toward the gray sedan waiting for her.

• • •

Luke pulled his red sports car behind Tyke's lifted black pickup. The team was using an abandoned bread factory as a meeting point. With cobblestone streets, an all brick front, and square tile windows, the structure was indicative of the forties era from when it had been built.

Water in the harbor gently lapped against the dock across the street. While the sun was bright enough to keep the water just above freezing, the sky held a gray tinge, reinforcing the impending harsh winter. It had already snowed twice this month, leaving behind a few inches on sidewalks and grassy areas. Meteorologists warned of more snow, a possible few feet, though no one seemed to be able to nail down exactly when. Not that it mattered. Even an inch was too much. The faster they solved this case, the faster he could end the threat on his life.

As Luke walked into the dimly lit room, the guys caught his movement through the doorway and turned.

"'Bout time," Ash Cooper said with a scowl, hands on his hips. "I almost had Reese GPS your phone." The DEA team leader looked like a damn cover model from one of Luke's foster mother's military romance novels. Strong jawline. High-and-tight haircut. Cargo pants. Black long-sleeved shirt with sleeves pulled up past his thick forearms.

Luke pulled a chair from the corner of the room, dragging the legs twenty paces across the bare concrete floor next to Bryan Tyke, who lounged in his own chair. There were days Tyke could be confused for either Chewbacca or Bigfoot. The beast of a man had a full beard and long dirty-blond hair pulled back with a hair tie. He wore a tightly fitted white T-shirt and camo pants with military boots. In other words, his Sunday best.

Jason Reese—the fourth member of the team—sat quietly at the other end of the table, wearing a simple long-sleeved shirt, flat-front pants, and small wire-frame glasses. He looked every bit like the cybersecurity geek he'd graduated as, rather than the DEA agent he was now. One leg kicked out in front of him, he reviewed footage on a video screen. Knowing Reese, it was probably the tenth time he'd been over that same footage. The guy was thorough and anal as shit.

"Seriously," Ash said. "Where the fuck were you? It doesn't take that goddamn long to get off. You stop for coffee and a biscuit with her this morning or what? You did go home with someone last night, didn't you? I'm assuming that's why you didn't answer your goddamn cell." It wasn't news that when Luke went to bars he usually ended up going home with a woman to her place, often leaving the morning after to meet the guys. However, taking a woman to Maybel's house and letting her sleep in his bed was a completely different story. He wasn't getting into all that with them because it didn't matter. It wasn't like Cassandra had stuck around or they'd see each other again.

Still would've been nice to talk a little more with her before she ran out of the house like it was wired to explode.

Which still boggled his mind.

Luke ran a hand over his short hair. "Just some complications this morning."

Ash did a double take, so did Tyke and Reese. Ash seemed to be fighting a smirk and losing miserably. "Complications? Since when does Luke Calder have complications with a woman? What happened? Couldn't close the deal? Stage fright?"

"She get a look at your tiny pecker?" Tyke said through a grin. "Or wait, let me guess—stage five clinger. Chick wouldn't let you leave her place because she thought the sex meant a relationship, flowers, and a ring."

All three men laughed.

Luke sat in his chair, clenching and unclenching his jaw. She'd left. Just like that. No explanation. Her phone made some kind of noise and then she bolted. He hadn't expected her to hang around forever, he hadn't wanted her to, but he'd at least planned to take her back to her place or wherever she needed. She hadn't given him that chance. And he wasn't really sure why that bothered him.

But it did.

Normally he was more than thrilled for a roll in the sack and a quick dash out the door. But he wasn't used to the *woman* being the one rushing out.

His mind started doing all sorts of tricks he didn't care for. He wondered where she'd ran off to. Where she lived. Where she was now. If she was okay. It was completely new territory for him. Usually it was *thanks for the amazing sex* and *let's do it again sometime*, knowing full well they'd never call each other. He preferred it that way.

He hadn't even slept with Cassandra, so why did he care so much that she was gone?

The men stared at him with raised eyebrows.

"Are we here to do a job?" Luke asked. "Or do you girls wanna braid each other's hair? Fill me in on what I missed."

Ash stared at him like he wanted to comment but didn't.

"Sure." He strode around the table and sat in a chair behind the largest video monitor, which displayed a vast snow-covered wooded area with a frozen pond. "Intel suggests the boys will be there today and they'll have some of the stash. Our objective is to confirm that Ronan is pushing drugs to minors. Once we receive solid confirmation, we move in."

Tyke bit into a chocolate-glazed donut, tearing half of it with his teeth, and said through the mouthful, "What about the gang? Don't we care that Ronan's recruiting kids and then they're dying?"

"We care about the drugs and the lives it's taking," Ash said.

"So if we find Serrano, we'll end the threat of death for those gang recruits."

José Serrano, responsible for creating some of the world's most addictive and dangerous drugs, was supplying the local-area gang with synthesized shit. Might not seem like a huge deal if a drug supplier was selling drugs to a gang, but the issue the DEA had was that the gang was recruiting kids from the neighboring high schools, and some of those recruits were dying after taking the drugs.

If the team caught Serrano, it would not only halt imports of the dangerous drug into Baltimore, but would also save the lives of hundreds of high school kids in the area. Plus, Luke had personal stake in this fight. He wanted to find Serrano ASAP. If he found Luke first, he'd kill him. Luke would prefer to see his thirty-first birthday this year.

So their task today was to watch two members of the gang, Ronan Cortez and Joaquin Estobar, as the pair met with a high school student interested in joining their gang. The hope was that they would offer up some sort of information that would lead the team to José Serrano.

"Reese, you've got stationary surveillance," Ash said, pointing at the monitor to a road on the side of the park.

"Tyke and Thor, ground coverage here." He gestured to an area above a giant frozen pond.

"Got it." Tyke looked down at his ninety-pound police dog sitting at his feet. "Don't we, boy?"

Thor barked his consent.

"Where do you need me?" Luke asked.

Ash tossed a camera with a high-powered lens at him. "Sam and I need engagement pictures."

"That's great. Back to the assignment, where do you—"

"That's your assignment," Ash replied. "Sam and I need engagement pictures. Or at least she says we do. You're a good photographer. That's our cover."

Luke glanced down at the black contraption in his hands, then back up at Ash. His best friend's expression didn't crack. "You're serious?"

"For all our sakes, don't screw this up."

BIOGRAPHY

Christina believes that laughter really is the best medicine, which is why in her stories she blends a healthy dose of hilarious hijinks with gritty suspense.

When she's not writing fun contemporary romance or quirky romantic suspense, Christina can be found devouring books in every genre, watching Chris Hemsworth on TV, playing board games with her family, working out, checking out Chris Hemsworth on Facebook, napping, stalking Chris Hemsworth on Instagram, and shopping…for Chris Hemsworth's latest DVD.

Christina lives near Baltimore with her husband and two sons, who give her an endless supply of humorous material to write about.

She is a member of Romance Writers of America and Maryland Romance Writers.

Want to be contacted when Christina has a new release or when her books go on sale?
Go here: https://goo.gl/forms/rhlyDE21Fv28PI6m1

Connect with Christina at:
www.ChristinaElleAuthor.com

OTHER BOOKS BY CHRISTINA ELLE:

ACKNOWLEDGEMENTS

Love always to my family first. Thanks to Keith for keeping the boys occupied while I spent every spare moment getting this finished.

To Misty for taking my half-assed ideas and transforming them into well-thought-out plots with strong conflict. And for your honesty and friendship.

To Jillian for reading this and catching my typos. Oh, and for laughing. I don't know if it's a good thing or a bad thing that you get my humor. But I'm thankful for it.

To Laura, who never makes me feel like a nag when I send a frantic email to her about all this self-publishing stuff. Thank you for your patience!

To you, the reader of this story or others I've written. Thank you for your time and feedback! I know life is busy, so it means the world that you chose to spend some of your time with my characters.

I'd be remiss if I didn't mention Chris Hemsworth. I mean, what Christina Elle novel doesn't talk about him somewhere, right? I might have used JJ Watt as inspiration for this story, but that's only because Chris hasn't starred in a film about football. In my mind, as I was writing this story, Chris's face was permanently attached to JJ's body. It was a glorious vision.

Thanks to Jessie, Kelly, and Jenna for a fun girls' weekend at the beach. My characters have a lot of work to do if they're going to keep up with you crazy broads. Love you! <3

47379749R00122

Made in the USA
San Bernardino, CA
12 August 2019